"So you've made your choice," *Brian said.*

Kate shook her head. "I've made no choices."

"Yes, you have. I told you I love you. And you can't say the words back. I tell you that I want to marry you, and you don't say yes."

"Brian—try to understand. Suddenly everyone says they want a part of me. They want to be part of my life."

He drew a hard breath. "Not me," he said in a firm voice.

She stared at him, tears bright in her eyes.

He fought the tenderness that made him want to accept anything she'd offer. "I don't want you just for this moment. I want you forever. And I don't want a part of you. I want all of your love."

"Brian!" she called out as he headed toward the door.

He stopped. So easily could he turn, pull her into his arms, be hurt again.

"Brian, it wasn't supposed to end like this."

Not turning around, he curled a hand around the doorknob. "It wasn't supposed to end."

Dear Reader,

Magic. It dazzles our senses, sometimes touches our souls. And what could be more magical than romance?

Silhouette **Special Edition** novels feature believable, compelling women and men in lifelike situations, but our authors never forget the wondrous magic of falling in love. How do these writers blend believability with enchantment? Author Sherryl Woods puts it this way:

''More. That's what Silhouette **Special Edition** is about. For a writer, this Silhouette line offers a chance to create romances with more depth and complexity, more intriguing characters, more heightened sensuality. In the pages of these wonderful love stories, more sensitive issues can be interwoven with more tenderness, more humor and more excitement. And when it all works, you have what these books are really all about—more magic!''

Joining Sherryl Woods this month to conjure up half a dozen versions of this ''special'' magic are Robyn Carr, Debbie Macomber, Barbara Catlin, Maggi Charles and Jennifer Mikels.

Month after month, we hope Silhouette **Special Edition** casts its spell on you, dazzling your senses *and* touching your soul. Are there any particular ingredients you like best in your ''love potion''? The authors and editors of Silhouette **Special Edition** always welcome your comments.

Sincerely,

Leslie Kazanjian, Senior Editor
Silhouette Books
300 East 42nd Street
New York, N.Y. 10017

JENNIFER MIKELS
Double Identity

Silhouette Special Edition

Published by Silhouette Books New York

America's Publisher of Contemporary Romance

SILHOUETTE BOOKS
300 East 42nd St., New York, N.Y. 10017

ISBN: 0-373-09521-X

First Silhouette Books printing April 1989

Books by Jennifer Mikels

Silhouette Special Edition

A Sporting Affair #66
Whirlwind #124
Remember the Daffodils #478
Double Identity #521

Silhouette Romance

Lady of the West #462
Maverick #487
Perfect Partners #511
The Bewitching Hour #551

JENNIFER MIKELS

has been a full-time writer for seven years. She started out an avid fan of historical novels, which eventually led her to contemporary romances, which in turn led her to try her hand at penning her own novel. She quickly found she preferred romance fiction, with its happy endings, to the technical writing she'd done for a public-relations firm. Between writing and raising two teenage boys, the Phoenix-based author has little time left for hobbies, though she does enjoy cross-country skiing and antique shopping with her husband.

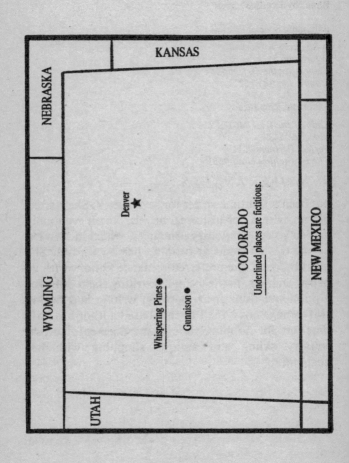

KANSAS

NEBRASKA

WYOMING

Denver ★

Whispering Pines ●

Gunnison ●

COLORADO
Underlined places are fictitious.

UTAH

NEW MEXICO

Prologue

Admirer or creep, he's been following me for days, and I don't like it.'' Katherine Lindstrom wrapped an arm around a grocery bag and lifted it from the checkout counter. "I'm not paranoid, Liz," she said as her neighbor grabbed the other bag. "Three times this week I've seen the same man."

Liz Claydell preceded her out the door. "A love-struck student?" she asked in her soft Southern drawl.

"At the age of five, students fall in love with their teachers. Add about twenty-five years to this one's age. And he's definitely not one of my students." Kate raised the collar of her winter coat.

"Tall, dark and handsome?"

"He appears to be. He's never gotten close enough for me to really see his face."

Liz raised her eyebrows. "You're kidding?"

"About what?"

"That he might be a tall, dark and handsome type?"

"I only have an impression," Kate said hastily. "Don't romanticize this."

"Would I do that?"

"You're in a vulnerable state."

Squinting as the snowflakes flew into her face, Liz attempted a glare. "If you mention the name Harry or any word that rhymes with it, I'm dropping this bag."

"Not me," Kate responded quickly, remembering Liz was carrying the bag with the eggs. "But how would you like it if some stranger was following you all the time?"

"You said you think he's good-looking."

"That doesn't exonerate a man from being a creep."

"I guess not," Liz said, wiping away the snow- flakes that had landed on the tip of her nose. "But why think dark thoughts?"

"What should I think?" Taking a shortcut to their apartment building, Kate led the way through the snowdrift.

"Mysterious strangers don't pop into every wom- an's life," Liz yelled at her back.

"I should be excited?"

"Why not? Any excitement is better than none."

"This isn't funny."

"You could be passing up James Bond."

"Or Jack the Ripper." Carefully Kate climbed the slick steps to the door.

"How tall is he?" Liz asked after they'd entered the narrow hallway that led to an inside door.

"Around six feet."

"How handsome?"

Kate rummaged through her purse. "Do you have your key for the inside door?"

"I always leave it in my mailbox."

"What if someone finds it?"

"Sometimes you're too cautious, Katie. So how handsome? A seven?"

"I told you that I didn't really see him. He wears a seaman's cap and a peacoat with the collar up around his face."

"But you have an impression," Liz persisted.

Kate dug into the bottom of her purse. Closing her fingers around the key, she looked back at the dark-haired woman whose nose was pointed toward the inside of the bag. "What's high?"

"Mel Gibson's a ten," Liz said absently.

"Maybe a nine."

Liz's head popped up. "Nine! He's a nine?"

"Physically. But he might be a one emotionally. Let's be serious."

"Are you going to the police then?" Liz followed her up the steps.

"And tell them what?"

"That a man is following you."

"Even you don't believe he's a threat, why would they?"

"Guess you're right." Liz shifted the bag to her other arm. "I have to go back to another store. Want to join me?"

Kate glanced at her wristwatch. "I'll pass. Rush hour traffic in Denver during a blizzard is strictly for people who like to punish themselves. Anyway, I want to bake cookies, and I have only a few hours before one of my students' fathers will arrive."

"Report card time?"

"Piano teachers don't give out report cards."

"So what's the problem?"

"Tommy Huntsbacker is feeling the pressure of having an overachiever for a father."

"Poor kid. Well, I'm off again by myself, then. I have no choice. I need balloons."

"Do you have a big party soon?"

"A small one. I'm catering a ritzy ten-year-old's birthday party. No one wants to have big parties anymore."

"No dark thoughts," Kate reminded her.

"You remember that, too. Think good ones about your mysterious stranger."

Kate nodded and turned away. Liz was definitely too trusting, she decided.

Brian Fleming stared at the apartment building a moment longer, then strolled down the street toward a two-story brownstone a block away. By the time he reached the top of the steps to his second-floor office, he'd shed the seaman's cap and his fleece-lined gloves and unbuttoned the peacoat. The sound of footsteps preceded his sister rounding the corner.

"I'm off," Sabrina announced. "Hold down the fort. I've got a lead on the runaway son." Two steps away, she whirled back. "Will you be around for a while?"

"An hour or two."

"Then what?"

"I'm going to talk to Lindstrom." Brian flipped up the collar of her coat. "It's cold out there."

"See you, big brother."

He nodded and then strode down the hall toward the office door of Fleming Investigations.

Chapter One

Two hours later Brian stood in the narrow entrance hall of the apartment building and searched for Lindstrom's name among the tags above a panel of buzzers.

"Are you looking for anyone in particular?"

At the feminine Southern drawl, he whirled around. "Katherine Lindstrom," he said, aware that he'd seen the tall, dark-haired woman with Lindstrom at the grocery store.

"She's expecting you."

Brian frowned. "She is?"

"Katie's my neighbor. I'm Liz." With one hand she whipped off a knit scarf dusted with snow while her other hand kept a tight grip on the strings of several balloons. "You can follow me in."

He tapped a finger at the panel of names above the row of buzzers. "She's not listed."

"Her name tag keeps slipping into the panel." She stepped around him to open her mailbox and fetch the key at the bottom.

"You shouldn't keep your key in the mailbox," he suggested as she unlocked the door.

She cast a look back at him and smiled wryly, but made no comment.

At the third-floor landing, the scent of freshly baked cookies greeted him. "What's her apartment number?"

"Follow the great smell. Last door. The one that's opened."

"Trusting soul, isn't she?"

He received no answer. Balloons bobbed against the ceiling as the woman strolled in the opposite direction.

Music floated through the hallway. Until that moment he hadn't noticed the sound of the piano. The music was highbrow. Brian paused at the doorway. Previously he'd viewed Katherine Lindstrom from a distance. He could offer a general physical description of her: a delicate blonde with dimples and great-looking legs. He'd noticed her legs. He'd liked her walk, the easy unhesitating fluidness of her stride.

Having followed her for days, he felt an intimacy with her. But then during the past few hours, he'd begun to believe that he'd been wasting his time trailing her. Still, he had a job to do and a client who wanted to know more about her.

A shaggy, tousled mane framed her heart-shaped face, accentuating her high cheekbones, her thin nose and her lightly tinted mouth. The eyes that raised and acknowledged him were a smoky blue, a blue that brought to mind the tip of a flame.

She stopped playing, and the sound of the final note of the Rachmaninoff concerto trailed off. As she rounded the piano, he yanked off his gloves and stared down at her pink sneakers with their chartreuse shoelaces. Not the stereotypical piano teacher, he mused as his attention shifted to her yellow sweatshirt. Printed on the front of it was a cartoon of Schroeder poised before his piano. Objectivity no longer seemed within Brian's grasp. He felt an interest stir. Then she smiled, and deep dimples appeared in her cheeks. A warning spark ignited within him.

He didn't look like an Alvin Huntsbacker to Kate. She'd expected a replica of the son, a fair, overweight boy. "I've been expecting you." She extended a hand while she fought a preoccupation with the deciphering quality in his dark blue eyes.

He remained standing in the doorway, his tall rangy build filling the space. Dark hair emphasized his dark eyes. She stared at his strong, angular face and the mouth that was so firmly drawn that it conveyed a silent message of stubbornness. He returned a smile that signaled puzzlement more than genuine friendliness.

"Is it getting colder outside?" she asked, in an attempt to break the ice.

"Yes."

"More snow?"

"Probably."

"I'm really glad that you decided to come and talk to me. Your son is such a great little boy."

"My son?"

"Not every child is musically inclined." Kate invited him in with a sweep of her hand. "And I work harder with those to show them the joy that they'll feel in making music," she went on. "Few people will become concert pianists, but that's not as important as the satisfaction a person will have in knowing how to play."

His eyes roamed over her, making her wish she'd changed out of the snug-fitting faded jeans. If he hadn't arrived so early, she'd have offered a different impression, she mused as he stared down at her sneakers. The jeans that he wore looked tailor-made, and his heavy jacket was a soft camel-colored cashmere.

"Is that why you think I'm here?"

Despite looks that she found attractive—too attractive—she felt a tinge of dislike for this man. She believed cold or indifferent fathers were as good as no father. "Well—yes. Sometimes though . . ." she noted a trace of amusement in his eyes. It annoyed her. She saw nothing humorous about why she'd requested a talk with him. "Sometimes parents expect more of a child than . . ."

He raised a halting hand. "Ms. Lindstrom."

Her name on his lips sounded harsh. Kate wished she could have a second to brace herself for the complaint he obviously planned to vent about his son's poor progress. "Mrs. Huntsbacker seemed to understand the problem."

A frown bunched his dark eyebrows.

"I don't ask the students. But with the divorce rate so high today, I never know if the child is with both parents or one of them."

He indicated only mild interest in what she was saying, his eyes settling on a print of a famous Andrew Wyeth painting.

"I didn't mean to probe," she said, insisting on his attention. "But if the divorce is recent or a painful one, it greatly affects a child's response to learning."

He gestured toward the painting. "This isn't an original, is it?"

Kate shook her head, but wanted to yell, *This is your son I'm talking about. Pay attention.*

"I always liked his work."

She clenched her jaw. "Actually, I didn't think Tommy's parents were divorced. Mrs. Huntsbacker brought him for his first lesson, but mentioned that it was you who was interested in having Tommy learn to play the piano." She directed a puzzled look at him, determined to force a response from him. "Mr. Huntsbacker...?"

Brian unbuttoned his jacket, preparing to reach back for his wallet. The charade had gone on long enough. He chided himself to get his foot out of his mouth, wondering why he'd deliberately stalled. "I'm not Huntsmucker," he announced abruptly.

"Hunts*backer*," she corrected. "You aren't? Then who..."

He shoved back his jacket and jammed a hand into his pants pocket. He saw panic flash into her gaze and realized for the first time that his small gesture could be menacing.

She narrowed her eyes as if pretending to view him from a distance. "Do you own a seaman's peacoat?"

"Yes, I do."

Her voice turned cold. "You're the one who's been following me?"

He noted that she'd skittered halfway to the telephone in less than two seconds. "Take it easy. I was doing a job. I didn't try to cover myself, so I assumed that when I came here and you invited me in that you'd recognized me."

"Recognized you? I don't even know you."

"No, I meant that I assumed you recognized me as the man who had been following you."

"We've established that." Her fingers curled around the telephone receiver. "Now, you'd better explain quickly who—"

"I'd planned to. My name is Brian Fleming." He flipped his wallet open. "I'm a private investigator."

She took a cautious step forward and tipped her head slightly to read his license. "Fleming Investigations?"

"Is something wrong?" Brian asked as she continued to stare at his license.

"How do I know that it's legitimate?"

"Why would you question it?"

"Because you don't look like a private investigator."

"What does one look like."

"Intense. And where—" The oven timer shrilled loudly, cutting her words short. "Excuse me for a minute."

Brian waited a second, then followed her into the kitchen. Small, the room was dominated by a maple table and straight-backed chairs. Like the living room, the kitchen was painted pale blue. Both rooms were decorated with antiques.

Her hand enclosed in a pot-holder mitt, she stood before the oven door and pulled out a baking sheet filled with golden-brown cookies. As he took a step farther into the room, she jumped. In less than a second, the cookies slid to one end of the pan, Brian lunged forward, she recoiled, and the pan was once again level.

For a long moment, breathing heavily, she simply stared at him, her irritation obvious. "I don't recall inviting you in here."

"I don't mind talking in the kitchen." He looked away to hide a grin. "It's kind of nice."

"Pushy, aren't you?"

"It's a necessary trait for my chosen occupation." Brian inhaled deeply. "Chocolate chip?"

"Yes." She set the pan on a cooling rack. "I thought I'd be done with these before you—Mr. Huntsbacker arrived."

"You probably will be."

"I really don't have to talk to you."

"No, you don't. But I'll be investigating you whether you do or not. So why not—"

"Cooperate?"

"Makes sense, doesn't it?"

"I don't understand. Who would want me investigated?"

Brian heard the nervous edge in her voice.

"Why me? I file my income tax yearly. I'm not seeing any married men. I've never even been married, so I couldn't have a husband looking for me. I don't have any outstanding traffic tickets. The only one I got was two years ago for parking in a no-parking zone."

He watched the denim strain across the tops of her slender thighs as she bent over to slide another baking sheet into the oven.

"I paid the ticket. And it wasn't my fault," she added, slamming the oven door. "Not really. I needed the sheet music for 'Ode to Joy' for a charity Christmas program."

"You were doing something charitable and ..."

"Got a ticket," she finished for him.

The irony had amused him. "Ms. Lindstrom..." he began, his lips slightly curved.

She set a plate of cookies on the table and grimaced.

"What's wrong?"

"You keep saying 'Ms. Lindstrom, Ms. Lindstrom.'"

"That's your name, isn't it?"

"Ms. Lindstrom sounds like some uptight, grayhaired woman with a thick Swedish accent."

"Katherine?"

"Kate," she said almost grudgingly.

He fought a smile.

"So who hired you?"

"For now, I can't disclose that."

Abruptly, she glared at him. "You can't?" A thoughtful look settled on her face, and she set a plate of cookies on the table. "Secrets drive me crazy. What do you want from me?"

"Information."

"Why?"

"A client of mine received a letter. Your name was mentioned."

"I know a lot of people. Was it a dissatisfied student complaining to ... ?"

"A woman named Dorothy Arneson wrote the letter."

A puzzled expression crossed her face.

"You know her, don't you?"

"Yes, I know her."

"She was the director at a private children's home north of Denver. The Piedmont."

"Was?"

"She's ill. Didn't you know that?"

"No. I haven't kept in touch with her."

"You were raised in the Piedmont, weren't you?"

"Yes. After my mother's death, I was sent there. It's like a boarding school. But I haven't seen Mrs. Arneson since I was eighteen. I suppose a great deal can happen in ten years." Questions clouded her eyes. "And now you say that she wrote a letter about me?"

"That's right."

"What did it say?"

"Mrs. Arneson claims that you might be a relative of my client."

A slip of a smile curved her lips. "Really?"

Brian measured her reaction. Surprise, a hint of pleasure. Either she was a great actress or he was totally confused. "Why the surprise?"

"I checked years ago. There aren't any other Lindstroms. At least none who were related to my mother. I'm surprised that Mrs. Arneson knew one of them and didn't say anything to me before I left the Piedmont."

"Lindstrom is your mother's last name?"

"I never knew my father's identity. His name wasn't on the birth certificate."

"My client's last name isn't Lindstrom."

She placed a hand on the back of one of the chairs and sat down slowly. "I'm not sure that I understand what's happening."

Brian felt lost in a fog of his own. "You lived at the Piedmont because you had no relatives?" At her nod, he questioned, "Why not an orphanage or a foster home?"

"There was money," she said distractedly. "An inheritance."

A dozen questions suddenly raced through his mind.

"The Piedmont is a private institution. Most of the children there had no relatives, but they did have trust funds and were placed there by executors of their families' estates."

Brian took a seat across from her. "This inheritance—how did you know that your mother left it?"

"Mrs. Arneson told me so."

"She just sat down one day and announced it?"

Her eyes narrowed at his skeptical tone.

"How old were you when you went to the Piedmont?"

"I don't ever remember not being there." She shoved the plate of cookies toward him. "I was brought there as a baby. I never knew my mother, either. And, as to your other question, I was about seven when Mrs. Arneson told me about the inheritance. There was a piano at the home. She saw me playing it—pounding on it—and realized I wanted to learn how to play. She told me then that I had the inheritance and that she would see that I received lessons with the money."

"Did you get more money later?"

"Yes, there was enough for college."

Brian sat back in the chair. "There was that much?"

"I also had a music scholarship."

Her hands were pale, long-fingered, delicately shaped. Her nails were manicured and polished with a clear gloss. He recalled the music she'd been play-ing when he'd arrived. He could imagine those hands moving caressingly across the keyboard. Soft hands. Gentle hands.

"Funny," she said mirthlessly, "I'm answering your questions, but you're doubting that I'm telling the truth, aren't you?"

He pretended a need to shift on the chair. Rows of miniature plants lined the long kitchen window. Yel-low daisies were everywhere—on the kitchen wallpa-per, in a vase on the table and even on the toaster cover. Daisies might suit her, he speculated. Sturdy yet delicate.

"No answer?"

"Right now I have more questions than answers. Do you give lessons here?"

"Yes."

"Don't your neighbors complain about the racket?"

"Music isn't racket."

"I have a sister who took piano lessons. Not every-one plays beautiful music."

"I have good neighbors," she said as an explana-tion. "They accept the music that comes from this apartment, and I . . ." She paused, tilting her head to the sound of a distant buzz. "That must be Mr. Huntsmuck—backer."

Brian pushed back his chair as she rushed from the kitchen to respond on the intercom. Disturbingly he realized that she wasn't what he'd expected. Too soft. Her manner lacked the hard edge of a woman who chose quick schemes to get rich. Was she just an in-nocent caught in the middle of something?

He strolled toward the door, but stopped suddenly. On the mahogany coffee table was a two-week-old newspaper. A headline caught his eye—it was the headline of a story about his client's relative. Why had Katherine Lindstrom saved it? Sudden questions bred doubts about her. Doubts, he realized, that the man in him wanted to ignore. Doubts that the investigator in him had to consider.

"It's Mr. Huntsbacker."

"I'll be leaving. I know it's none of my business, but don't you think that you should keep your door closed? Locking it wouldn't hurt, either. Or are you that trusting?"

"My buzzer is broken." An exotic scent assailed him as she passed him in the doorway. "What do you plan to do now?" she asked suddenly.

"Ask more questions."

"Check out my story?"

"It's the usual procedure."

"Don't I have any choices?"

Brian frowned. "What do you mean?"

"I'm not sure that I want to know what you learn."

"Why wouldn't you want to know?"

"Because after all these years, some relative might suddenly crawl out of the woodwork and announce that I'm a dear lost relative. Where was that person years ago?"

Brian heard hurt and a tinge of bitterness. "If that's true, it's entirely up to you what you do, isn't it?"

Was it? Kate wondered as they silently descended the steps. At the familiar squeak of the inside door closing two landings below them, she set aside questions. Mr. Huntsbacker was at the bottom of the stairs, she reminded herself. She needed to present a calm, confident image to him. But another man had unexpectedly upset her life. She looked back at him. "There's a loose step," she warned.

Head bent while he buttoned his jacket, he looked up puzzled. "What?"

"The step," Kate repeated. At an image of him flying forward and tumbling down the steps, she whirled around. Her foot reached the wobbly step at the same moment as his. She didn't think. Instinctively, she yanked him toward her. His weight shifted, and he fell hard on top of her, pushing her back up against the banister.

They stood in an awkward embrace, his one arm flung around her hip, his other tight at her shoulder in a protective clinch. His leg was intimately wedged between hers. She tilted back her head and looked at his face, at his slow smile.

"You're full of surprises."

"The step," she responded, struggling to think and to sound calm while she convinced herself that her legs didn't feel weak.

"What about the step?"

"The edge of it is loose."

"Loose?"

Kate nodded, aware her breasts were flattened against him. "You would have hurt yourself coming down on it so fast."

"So you rescued me?"

"Yes, I guess I did."

"Nice of you."

"My pleasure."

Still pressed close against her, he smiled broadly. "No, I definitely believe it's mine."

He was a stranger, a disruptive force, she mused, but undeniably attractive. She accepted her feelings for what they were—sexual. Attractive. A dull description, she decided, staring at his eyes. Much more than just attractive.

"In some countries what you did would mean that I belong to you now."

"Belong?"

"You may have saved my life."

"Nothing so dramatic."

"It depends on how you view it."

"And you view it as . . . ?"

"Saving my life."

When he stepped back, no longer trapping her, Kate grabbed a sturdy hold on the banister. Her legs felt wobbly beneath her.

He descended two steps, then stopped. His warm grin was gone. "I'll be back," he said, so deadly serious that her nerves instinctively jumped again.

A second passed before she noticed another man. Short, heavy and fair, he frowned, reminding her of a disgruntled Shih Tzu. "Mr. Huntsbacker?"

"Yes."

"I was expecting you."

"I've been expecting you." Brian's sister rounded the desk with quick strides. "What took you so long?"

Brian nudged her elbow in passing, pushing one fist off her hip.

"So where have you been?" Sabrina trailed behind him as he strolled toward his desk.

"Talking to Katherine Lindstrom."

"Why the scowl? Isn't the investigation going well?"

"I'm having doubts about our client's motive."

"Brian, don't ponder too much. It always gets us in trouble."

He looked up from an unopened manila file folder.

"Gertrude Stranton is an important client. One megabucks client could mean more of the same if we do a good job. Think of the referrals."

"They'd be great. But don't you wonder why our agency was contacted?"

Sabrina frowned. "What's wrong with us?"

"We're a rinky-dink operation in comparison to some investigative agencies."

"Maybe she heard that we're the best."

Brian laughed. "You're our best endorser."

"What's the problem?"

"A woman who doesn't know her father's identity," he said.

"Katherine Lindstrom?"

"Yes. And I—"

"What does she look like?"

"What does that matter?" He sorted through the mail.

His sister tilted her head. "What does she look like?"

He ignored the question. "I can't figure her out."

"Do you think she's involved in a scam?"

"Could be. Her or Arneson. Or both." He thought again about the newspaper he'd seen on the coffee table. She'd acted as if she'd known nothing about the letter. But then why had she kept that particular issue? he wondered. He'd been an investigator too many years to allow his libido to blind him to the fact that some beautiful women walked on the shady side of life. "I followed Lindstrom for days. I thought there might be a silent male partner involved in some scheme."

"No boyfriend?"

"Didn't see one lurking around a corner."

"What did Arneson demand for the information that she gave Gertrude Stranton about Lindstrom?"

"Nothing."

"Out of the goodness of her heart she sent Stranton information that Lindstrom might be a relative?"

"That's right." He tapped a pencil on the edge of the desk in a syncopated beat. "Only our client isn't playing the game straight with us."

"Why?"

"Because Katherine Lindstrom doesn't know and has never known who her father was." Brian raised his eyes. "So do we have a scam by Lindstrom and Arneson? Or do we have a cover-up about an illegitimate child to prevent scandal?"

"Both are possible."

"Yeah. Isn't wealth wonderful? Those who have it use it to play games with another person's life. And those who don't have it will do anything to get it."

"Brian, your objectivity is slipping."

"No, it isn't. The game is called 'deception.' I just don't know who the players are yet. The only thing I'm sure of is that all of this has to do with money."

Sabrina pushed away from the desk. "You have a tainted view of wealthy people. Forget Diane."

Brian bent to the side and reached into his bottom desk drawer for a Tootsie Roll. "I have."

Sabrina sent him a dubious look and whirled away.

While he unwrapped the candy, he saw her slip a can of Mace from her desk drawer and into her purse. "Where are you going?"

"To track down that runaway."

"Where?"

"In a less-than-desirable neighborhood."

"Brie, I could go..." Her glare stopped him. "Forget I even started that sentence. 'But know what's ahead of you before you take a step,'" he said, spouting one of his father's warnings. He wished Thomas Fleming had always practiced what he'd preached.

He saw a flicker of grief cloud her eyes for a second. With a turn of her dark head, she threw back a sunnier look. "And you be careful."

"I will," he answered, but wondered if the warning had come too late. During that brief encounter with Kate Lindstrom, he'd felt an interest stir within him and sparks ignite when her softness had pressed against him. He'd felt a temptation to kiss her.

Chapter Two

As the setting sun glared through the slats of the blind in his office, Brian cradled the telephone receiver between his jaw and shoulder and then yanked on the Venetian blind's cord. It wouldn't budge. "Do you want to play straight with me, Mrs. Stranton?"

"Try to understand, Mr. Fleming," the woman responded stiffly. "I had no idea if this was some scheme produced by this young woman and this Mrs. Arneson to wheedle money out of me."

"Her story checks out. I spent part of the morning going through vital statistics. Her birth certificate verifies what she told me."

"What does this woman seem like?"

"Confused. And so am I, Mrs. Stranton." Brian gave the cord a hard yank, then jumped back as the blind fell from the window. It hit the top of the desk with a clatter. Swallowing a curse, he mumbled an apology. "Sorry."

"What happened?"

"Something fell. Mrs. Stranton, do you have any Lindstroms in your family?" At her negative response, he persisted, "Do you believe that she could be from your side of the family?"

A long second passed before she replied, "I don't know. Of course, anything is possible, but I—the Higgens family tree was traced years ago."

He was aware that the family lineage dated back to the American Revolution. His client was still dancing around him. "If you want me to stay on this case, then I plan to disclose your name to her."

Panic sounded in the woman's voice. "Why?"

"I need to see her reaction to your name."

Silence answered him.

"It's the best way to smoke her out."

"I beg your pardon."

"Do you object to her knowing your name?" he asked.

"Is it wise to do that?"

"It's the logical thing to do. And you have to decide now. How far do you want me to investigate this?"

"I'm not sure that I fully comprehend what you're asking me."

"Katherine Lindstrom just may be a relative of yours. If she isn't involved in any criminal act, do you want me to pursue this and dig up the past?"

"Wouldn't she insist on it?"

"I'm not so sure that she would."

"I find that difficult to believe."

"She seemed more reluctant to accept some long-lost relative than you are."

"Is she really?"

"I said that she *seems* to be that way."

"Yes, I see. You understand my reluctance. I was shocked to receive that letter. I had never heard of her mother, this Madeline Lindstrom. And we don't know yet if Katherine Lindstrom is lying."

"No, we don't." He gathered the blind together and jammed it into a wastebasket. "So what do you want me to do?"

"Continue. If she is one of our own, I need to know."

"All right."

"You'll talk to her again?"

"I planned to."

"I'll rely on your judgment then, Mr. Fleming. If it's what you want to do..."

No, it wasn't what he wanted to do, he thought. What he wanted to do was forget the case. He didn't care who her relatives were. But she definitely interested him.

He knew he should hand the case over to Sabrina. He also knew that he wouldn't.

Before dawn the next day, Brian parked in front of Kate Lindstrom's apartment building. An arm draped over the steering wheel, he squinted against the bright sunlight and stared up at her apartment windows. Since dawn, one curtain had been opened. For all he knew, she might spend all day inside. He sipped the muddy-looking coffee that he'd bought at a fast-food restaurant and then punched numbers on his car telephone.

The phone rang only once before Tom Malone answered. "Malone, vice."

"Hey, Detective Malone, do you feel like doing a friend a favor?"

"I'm not tapping the police computer into FBI files for you."

"Did I ask?" Brian yawned.

"Doing surveillance work again?"

"Yeah. Would you check your records there for me?"

"Who is it?"

"Well—two people."

"Two?"

As she emerged from the apartment building, Brian sat up. "Katherine Lindstrom."

"You're going to owe me an explanation later."

"Okay," he replied, watching her lower her head against the wind. Then, stubbornly she lifted her chin. "And another woman, Dorothy Arneson."

"Spell the last names."

He complied while turning on the ignition. "Find out anything you can. Anything," he said, easing the car into the street to follow her.

Twenty minutes later Brian braked several yards from where she'd parked, but he knew she'd been aware of his car. Unlike some cases, he hadn't kept a low profile during this one. Sometimes his high visibility unnerved amateurs, and they gave up their criminal pursuit. Despite the stirring of his blood when he'd been with her, he believed in the power of reason above all else. Good sense cautioned him to keep his mind on business. Not always was that an easy task.

Her head high, she stormed toward his car as if prepared to do battle. Nice walk, he thought again, and waited until she rapped on his car window before rolling it down.

"What are you doing here?"

"My job."

"Not today." Her tone wavered between an appeal and a demand.

Brian watched her march away and disappear inside a small theater. He waited for a few seconds, then followed. The billboard advertised evening performances of a children's concert. But with a glance he noted that the parking lot was empty except for one car. He yanked open the theater door. Who was she meeting? Rushing inside to escape the cold, he came face-to-face with her.

"Please, leave me alone today," she said, her voice low.

He scanned the empty auditorium. "Why are you here?"

"Now, you look. I've tried to be pleasant. But you're making me feel like a criminal. And what's more important is that you're going to ruin everything for me with Boris—"

"Boris? Who's Boris? Friend or lover?"

"That's none of your business. In fact, nothing I do is any of your business. You're going to ruin everything."

"Everything what?"

"If you don't leave me alone, I'll call the police and get one of those—those . . ."

"A restraining order," Brian supplied.

"Yes, one of those."

Brian looked past her. A man approached them. Though no taller than five-foot-five, he was a barrel of a man with a square jaw. Jowls made his face appear even larger.

Nervously, she glanced back. "Now what am I to do? If he asks who you are, what do I tell him?"

Brian couldn't imagine the slender young woman before him caught in an erotic clinch with the gray-haired man steps away from them. "Who is he?"

"Boris Breshkov. He has a very exclusive music academy."

"I know." Five years ago the newspaper had had a field day with the Russian maestro's defection.

"I would like to get a position with his academy. And you're here."

"Teaching?"

"You could cost me that chance."

He touched her hand. If felt like ice. Playing the heavy had never suited him. He squeezed her hand reassuringly. "I won't."

"Miss Lindstrom. How nice to see you."

She whirled around with a tight smile.

"Thank you for coming here. It must be an inconvenience to come to the theater rather than my studios, but, as you know, I have limited time for instructor auditions."

"It wasn't any problem. Really."

"What composition have you decided to play for me?"

"Chopin. Opus 24."

"You choose wisely."

As Breshkov's gaze turned on Brian curiously, he extended a hand. "Brian Fleming, sir."

He gripped Brian's hand, but continued to scowl.

Aware the ball was in his court, Brian reached out and slid her car keys from Kate's fingers. "Thanks,

Katherine, for letting me borrow your car. I'll have it back by the time you're done." He ignored her wide-eyed, almost panicked expression and walked away with her car keys dangling from his hand. If looks could kill, he would have been inhaling his last breath.

Waiting was a part of his job that he'd never liked. But he couldn't remember time ever passing so pleasantly before. Standing at the door, he listened to the sweeping notes of the lone piano. He didn't need to see her. Her music surrounded him, waves of sound crashing and ebbing, floating through the air. He leaned back against the wall and closed his eyes, breathless as he listened to the sustained melody, the astounding sequence of chords, the crescendo at the finish. He sensed her dedication. He felt her passion—her love for music.

As the music stopped, he went outside and ambled to the curb. A teenage boy started to cross the street, then stepped back onto the sidewalk and bent over to pack snow between his bare hands. A snowball sailed across the street and brushed the shoulder of a curvy, adolescent girl.

Smiling, Brian looked down and scribbled a thought on the pocket-size notebook in his hands. As if preparing him for another woman's approach, a South Seas fragrance drifted toward him on the cold air. Head erect, shoulders back, she looked beautiful but uncertain, despite the proud stare she directed at him. He noted the fire was gone from her eyes, replaced by a coolness he found just as intriguing.

Kate held her hand out in front of him. "My keys."

"How did it go?" he asked, ignoring her palm.

"Great, no thanks to you. I suppose you've come with more questions."

"In a way."

"You have a unique and irritating habit of answering questions with fragments."

"I could pretend that I'm here for that reason."

"Another full sentence. Wonderful."

"Or I could pretend that I came to keep an eye on you."

"But there's another reason. Right?"

"Yes. A simple one."

"What is it?"

"I thought you'd like to know the name of my client."

"Why the sudden change? A couple of days ago you acted as if it was a secret that you'd withstand torture for."

"I needed permission."

"From your client?"

"Yes. She'd requested that I keep her name a secret."

"She?" Kate frowned, realizing that she'd assumed his client was a man. Perhaps her father. She suddenly felt besieged by mixed feeling of disappointment and relief. "How—how did you change her mind?"

"It's obvious, isn't it?"

She stared down at her boots. Baffled, she gave him a quizzical look. "You've told me that I'm being investigated, and now you and she have decided to reveal her name." She shook her head. "I don't understand. Who is she?"

"Gertrude Stranton hired me."

"I don't know anyone by that name."

The eyes staring at her were intense. She'd been wrong, he did have that purposeful, hard look. She'd allowed the charming smile and mischievous sparkle in his eyes to fool her and make her believe that the word *dangerous* didn't suit him. But it did.

"You've never heard of the Strantons?"

"No, I don't know the..." She paused. "Wait a minute. That name does sound familiar."

"If you read the newspaper—"

She glared at him. "I do."

"The Stranton name was in it recently."

"I don't read the society page."

"What makes you believe that's where it was?"

"People without money don't hire private detectives, do they?"

"Sharp deduction." He grasped her elbow and urged her across the street. "You're right. The Stranton name is frequently mentioned in the society section. But they also made front page recently. Gertrude Stranton's brother-in-law Edward died of a heart attack two weeks ago."

"Senator Stranton? Of course," Kate said softly. "That's why the name sounded familiar..." Her voice trailed off, and she froze in midstride. "Wait a minute. You're kidding, aren't you?"

"No." He unlocked the car door for her. "Arneson claimed that you might be a relative of the Strantons."

"That's ridiculous. They—I..." Brian watched a frown crease her forehead. "What does she—Gertrude Stranton—want from me?" she asked.

"To find out if someone wants something from her?"

"Someone?"

Brian waited for her eyes to meet his.

"I don't understand you. You never tell me anything, really—just little comments. You make me feel as if you've dropped one shoe, and I'd better be ready for the thump of the second."

"Conveniently the letter arrived two weeks after the senator died."

Her back straightened. "What do you mean, conveniently?" Her eyes met his now with a steady gaze that might have nailed a lesser man's back to a wall. "If you're insinuating—"

"My job is to get the truth, not make up lies."

"Well, the truth is that I don't know your client, and quite honestly I don't want to. And I don't know why Mrs. Arneson would write a lie like that, why she would hurt me this way."

"Good question. Why would she?"

"You're a difficult man to like."

"Am I?"

"Yes. And I've had enough." She started to push past him.

He snapped a hand over her wrist. "Easy," he soothed. "I'm not trying to upset you."

"Of course, you're not."

"Maybe, a little. Anger sometimes unsettles people, and truth slides out on rash statements."

"I've told you that I don't know anything about any letter. And I'm puzzled. Why would your client even pay any attention to that letter? Or aren't you allowed to tell me that? I mean, you do work for someone else, so would that be a conflict of interest if you answered my questions?"

Brian ran his thumb over her wrist, unsure if he'd bruised her with his tight grasp. But he'd wanted to stop her. He wanted this woman to be innocent of any wrongdoing. Still, one piece of unexplained evidence continued to plague him with doubts.

"Isn't this sort of thing—investigating—usually done on the sly? Sort of like amateur-spy stuff?"

"Where did you get that idea?"

"From the movies."

"Life isn't like the movies," he said shortly. "Not all heroes live. Not all romances end in happily ever after." He regretted the comments instantly. She had to have heard his bitterness. Blame it on grief, he wanted to say. Grief for a father who was loved. And grief for a wife who never loved.

"So whenever you investigate someone, you tell them that you're doing it?"

"This isn't turning into a normal investigation," he admitted, rubbing his thumb across the underside of her wrist. It felt as soft as velvet. "But if the letter is part of a deceptive scheme, then confronting you is the fastest way to end it."

"So, sight unseen, your client doesn't trust me?"

"Doesn't know you, either."

Her brow knitted in a puzzled expression.

He felt an urge to trace her forehead, to touch her skin, to kiss her and to say to hell with the job.

"You don't trust me, either. Why? Because you hate my chocolate-chip cookies? Because you think I play the piano miserably? You don't know me beyond that, so why would you—"

"I saw a two-week-old newspaper in your apartment."

"An old newspaper?"

"On the coffee table. Up until that moment I really didn't think you were involved. I have no idea if Arneson is telling the truth or not. But I assumed that you didn't know anything about the letter that Mrs. Stranton had received."

"But then you saw the newspaper," she said in slow, measured words, as if questioning his logic.

He watched the sunlight play across her face, casting the edge of her lips and the curve of her jaw in shadow. As she bent her head in thought, the pale strands of her hair looked like silk. He wondered if they'd feel as soft. He was losing perspective, he reminded himself. Objectivity had gone out the window during their initial meeting. But in fairness to Gertrude Stranton, he couldn't let his preoccupation, his attraction for this woman, keep him from pursuing and challenging. "That newspaper carried a follow-up story about Senator Stranton's death."

"And that convinced you I was guilty?"

"Why did you keep that newspaper?"

She looked away.

"Hey?"

Her eyes sparkled with amusement.

"Why do I get the feeling now that something has happened and I'm the only one who doesn't know about it?"

"Oh, I doubt that," she replied, but he heard an airy quality in her tone. "Very few people are aware of who we are. That you're a private investigator or that I'm a music teacher. That you believe I should be locked up—"

"I didn't say that," he returned fiercely.

She shrugged and turned her face from him.

Brian felt that he was being baited, but he didn't know what was on the hook.

"Obviously you have not investigated me thoroughly enough to find out that I'm quite pleased with most of my students. Proud of them." She met his gaze again. "One in particular. Tricia Farnello. She won an award, Most Promising Young Pianist of the Year. Maybe, you read about her."

"In the newspaper?"

She nodded.

"When? Two weeks ago?"

She nodded again.

He released a hearty sigh. "Damn."

"Do you jump to conclusions often?"

Not usually, he wanted to say. But usually his mind never strayed from business, never wondered about a woman's perfume or what her laugh sounded like.

"It's probably another one of those necessary traits for your job."

Her tease helped him. "Not necessary, but I'm definitely stuck with it."

She slid into the car.

Brian curled a hand over the top of the door to halt her from closing it. "Congratulations."

"Thank you. She's an excellent student."

He stared at the deep curve of a dimple in her cheek. He stared at her lips and felt the hard thud of his heart. Time stood still. One taste, he told himself. One kiss and he'd be satisfied.

He closed the door. Who was he kidding? he mused as he strolled toward his car. During that one second when she'd smiled at him, he'd sensed that one kiss wouldn't be enough. He wanted to make love to her.

He wanted to know the passion within her, the passion he'd heard in her music.

Not wanting to give herself time to worry about the audition or to think about Brian Fleming, Kate spent the rest of the morning cleaning closets and dusting. As she swiped a rag across the piano keyboard, Liz appeared in her doorway.

"Your Mr. Huntsbacker was quite a fox."

"He wasn't."

"You're blind."

Kate turned a quizzical look on her. "How do you know what he looked like?"

"I let him in."

"Oh, Liz." Kate felt a giggle tickling her throat. "He wasn't Mr. Huntsbacker." She turned down the stereo volume to quiet a wailing Springsteen.

"Who was he?"

"He was—is the man who's been following me."

"Your nine?" Liz shifted a round freezer carton from one arm to the other. "So what did he want? Who is he?"

Kate tapped a fingernail at the freezer carton. "First, tell me what's in that carton?"

"Spumoni." Liz gave her a Cheshire-cat grin. "For us."

"It's eleven in the morning."

"So?"

"You want me to indulge in spumoni at eleven in the morning?"

"Not really. What I really want is some of your chocolate-chip cookies. I brought the spumoni, hoping you'd share your cookies."

"*You* needed the spumoni."

Liz made a grudging admittance. "Okay, *I* needed the spumoni."

"Harry came by?"

"He called." Liz waved a hand to halt Kate. "I don't want to talk about him. Tell me who Mr. Nine is?"

"A private investigator."

Liz hissed loudly. "That lousy Harry. What is he up to now?"

"This had nothing to do with Harry. I swear, Liz, you're getting—" Kate rocked her hand.

Liz laughed. "You're right, I am. So if Harry didn't hire this guy to get something on me, then . . . ?"

"He's investigating me," Kate informed her, unable to veil her disbelief at the idea. "Come in the kitchen and I'll tell you the story."

Ten minutes later, Kate had divulged the story and was scraping a spoon along the bottom of the ice-cream dish. "Do you think any of this is true?" Liz asked.

"I don't know." Kate pushed back her chair to reach the coffeepot. "Right now none of it makes sense to me."

"Your problem is you're like me. Truth is important," she mumbled. "We both believe that."

The pain in Liz's voice alerted Kate. She paused in pouring the coffee into the cups. "What's the latest on Harry?"

"Simply said, he's a pain in the—"

"Neck," Kate supplied.

Liz raised hazel eyes. "I had a different part of the anatomy in mind."

"When did you talk to him?"

Liz smoothed one errant frosted strand away from her face. "Last night. I wish that I could tell him to take a flying leap somewhere, but seven years of marriage is hard to forget. Mid-life crisis," she scoffed.

"Harry's only thirty-six. Seven-year itch."

"Whatever it is, it's something I'd have been delighted to never experience."

"Do you hate men now, Liz?"

"All of them."

"Every single one?"

Liz's shoulders heaved measurably. "I'm a terrible liar, huh?"

Kate touched her friend's shoulder. "Yep."

"He made me so angry. When he announced that he was moving out centuries ago—"

"About a month ago."

Liz propped an elbow on the table and rested her jaw on her palm. "Yes. Well, then he said that he wanted some space. Space! A today term used as an excuse to be free to mess around."

"What did he say last night that upset you so much?"

"He loves me."

Kate frowned.

"Isn't that a corker," Liz said, sliding her glasses onto the bridge of her nose. "At thirty-three, I have a husband who's suddenly developed arrested adolescence. He seems to want whatever he doesn't have."

"Then what's the problem?" Kate asked. "Why didn't you and he . . . ?"

"Kiss and make up?" At Kate's nod, Liz murmured, "Because I know there's another woman. There has to be. Otherwise, why did he insist on space. For years he was too busy for me. Harry Claydell is a workaholic and will always be one. Lawyers can always find a criminal. But now, suddenly, he seems to have all kinds of time to furnish a new apartment and look for women and still bug me.''

Kate handed her another cookie.

"I'm not good at sharing," Liz added. She held her hands out in an appealing gesture. "So what do I have, Katie? A man who wants to find himself. Thirty-six years old and he doesn't know who he is?" She pushed her glasses back.

"Could be that he's come to his senses."

"I'm not sure that I want him."

Kate didn't argue; the same kind of pride made her angry every time she thought about Brian Fleming's investigation. For too many years she'd longed for someone to claim her, to make her part of a family. She'd thought that she'd left that need in her past. But had she? she wondered.

"Do you understand that?"

Kate nodded. "I understand," she replied loudly, trying to be heard over the ringing telephone.

"A student with an unexpected bellyache?" Liz teased in advance.

"No, my late appointment is with a seventy-year-old man who's bound and determined to play 'Sweet Adeline' to his wife for their fiftieth anniversary." Kate took a quick swallow of coffee before answering the phone, "Hello?"

"Kate—Kate Lindstrom?"

"Yes," she answered, afraid to place the familiar male voice.

"Brian Fleming. I'd like to stop by later this evening."

Kate pressed a hip against the stove.

"Will you be home?" he asked, seeming not to notice her lack of response. "If you were going out . . ."

"No, I wasn't."

"If you're free for dinner, we could . . ."

"Dinner?" Kate held back the receiver and looked at Liz.

"Who is it?" Liz whispered. "Never mind, whoever it is, say yes."

Kate frowned and turned her back to Liz. "I have a student coming."

"After?"

She suspected he was smiling. Disturbingly, she recalled the way his lips curved in a slow, sexy grin.

"Your silence is killing my ego."

She struggled to abate a laugh.

"There's an Italian restaurant near your apartment, isn't there?"

"Yes."

"We could go there."

"I won't be done until after eight."

"Is he a good student?"

"Yes, he's very good."

"Couldn't he have time off for excellence? Dinner," Brian said appealingly, "a pleasant repast with congenial conversation."

Kate curled the cord around her finger. The man was turning her world into a chaotic state. "No," she answered quickly before she changed her mind.

"It doesn't matter how late."

"No."

"Tomorrow?"

She nearly laughed.

"Does silence mean that your answer is still no?"

"Yes."

"Yes to what I said? Or yes it means no?"

"It means no."

"The next evening?"

"Another student."

"What about the following—"

"No time would be right for me," she replied, and replaced the receiver in its cradle before he could say more.

"What was that all about?" Liz asked.

"Sam Spade wanted to go out to dinner."

Liz cracked a smile. "And you turned him down?"

"I did."

"Why? He's young, handsome, has a steady job. And from what I could hear, he had a sense of humor. Maybe even a little charm."

"As much as a bulldozer has."

"Why didn't you, Katie?"

"Because I don't like what he might do to my life."

"You don't want him finding out if you have any relatives?"

"I didn't ask him to, did I?"

"No."

"But if I see him, then won't he feel compelled to tell me what he's learned?"

Liz nodded.   A decent sort would."

"That's why I said no."

"Because he's a decent sort?"

"Yes."

Liz's voice brightened. "You're attracted to him."

Kate glowered at her. "Eat the cookies."

"You don't want to be." Liz's dark eyebrows pinched together. "Why not?"

In an effort to avoid answering, Kate crammed a cookie into her mouth.

Chapter Three

Three days later Brian told himself that he'd needed distance from Kate. If what he sensed stirring for her was a simple physical attraction, he could handle it. But he couldn't analyze anything—not his feelings or his reasons or his obsession to see her again. He only knew that his infatuation had nothing to do with the investigation.

He'd weighed the information he'd gotten from Kate and from Gertrude Stranton. But he needed to talk to Dorothy Arneson.

Around him, bowling balls rumbled down the alleys. Though pins flew beneath the velocity and force of his ball, the seven pin remained standing. Turning, he shrugged at Tom Malone.

"Are you trying to kill the pins?"

"You win this game," Brian conceded. "I owe you a beer."

"What's bugging you?" Tom asked.

Brian sat on the curved bench beside his friend and bent forward to untie his bowling shoes. He'd been hired to do a job, and all he could think about was protecting the woman he was supposed to investigate. Though he'd managed to stay away from her, he was losing the battle. "A case that I'm working on."

"Want to talk about it, lad?"

Brian grinned at his friend. "Whenever I have a problem, why do you always sound as if you're trying out for Barry Fitzgerald's priestly role in *Going My Way*?"

"Loved that movie. Tugged me heart." Tom shoved his shoes into a bag. "Make it a friendly talk then and I'll offer you my worldly wisdom."

"Off the record, Detective," Brian insisted.

"You even have to question that?"

"What about honor and duty before all else?" Brian asked in a a teasing tone.

"Lay off. That's the mumbo jumbo I get from your sister all the time," he said as they strolled toward the adjacent bar. "So what's your latest problem?"

"Conscience."

Tom grimaced. "About Katherine Lindstrom? Twenty-eight-year-old music teacher whose driver's license photo is probably taped to some motor vehicle department employee's wall? And drooled over," he added.

"That's the one. It's possible that she's a close relative of the Strantons."

"*The* Strantons?"

"Are there any others?"

"How close?"

"Close."

"When we talked last, you mentioned that she might be involved in something." As they reached the bar, Tom signaled the bartender.

"That was before you checked the files and came up empty-handed."

"No criminal record," Tom assured him.

"And I stopped considering that some guy was hiding in the closet."

"Two beers," Tom yelled out. He swiveled his stool toward Brian. "Oh, I see where you were headed. The theory of female led astray by masterful man?"

"She wouldn't be the first woman to be courted into a life a crime."

"What conclusions have you reached?"

"I haven't."

"That's slow for you." He offered the bowl of peanuts to him.

Brian shook his head. "I don't want anything to eat. Something isn't right."

"Like what?"

"Gertrude Stranton hiring an investigator. Not telling her husband about doing it."

"Skeletons rattling in the closet?"

"Something like that."

Tom cracked a nut. "Didn't you meet the Strantons when you were married to Diane?"

"Yes."

"Well, you know why she chose your agency then."

"Sharing pâté doesn't develop kinship."

"Since you did rub elbows with her and her husband at a party, she might have thought you'd be a discreet investigator for them."

Brian nodded. A vivid recollection flashed through his mind. Tempers had flared between Diane and him right before they'd left home for that party. He'd gone to it with her that evening. The next day she'd left with friends for Bermuda, all expenses paid by Diane's father.

"And you have been discreet," Tom said in a curious tone. "Except for names, you haven't told me much of anything."

"I plan on keeping it that way."

"So what does your conscience have to do with this case? With Lindstrom?"

"I'm trying to uncover information that will be difficult for her to handle. Even if I learn nothing, I'll reopen old wounds."

Tom sent him a worried look. "I thought one of the rules in your business was never to get involved with a client."

"She isn't my client."

"You're skirting the issue."

Brian frowned. Tom's comments were complicating everything. "I'll get the job done."

Tom slurped foam from his beer. "I never doubted that. I'm going to the Shamrock. Want to come along?"

Brian glanced at his watch. "No. I have something else to do. Ask your uncle to save me a bowl of mulligan stew."

"I avoid Uncle Charley at his restaurant. If he's short help, he drafts me to clean tables."

"That I'd like to see."

"I bet."

"Are you on the graveyard shift again?"

"Best time for the vice squad. Midnight to six in the morning."

"Keeps you out of other trouble." Brian slid off the stool and plunked money on the bar.

"Where are you going at nine-thirty in the evening?"

"An aerobics class."

For the past three weeks Kate had forced herself to go to the neighborhood health club once a week. Her muscles still rebelled at the self-imposed Tuesday-night punishment. As she strolled from her car and into the grocery store across from her apartment building, she felt an ache in her calf. If exercise made a person feel better, why did she always feel so lousy while doing it? she wondered as she strolled down an aisle of stacked cans.

Briefly she hesitated, then tossed a bag of spice drops into her grocery cart before moving to the counter that displayed grapes.

"Do you spend all your spare time in grocery stores?"

She didn't need to look at the man. Brian Fleming had a distinctive voice. Low, a touch raspy, it was a whiskey voice. Defensively, she straightened her back to prepare herself for the next few moments. He kept dropping in and out of her life, and on every occasion he'd left her feeling baffled or unsteady. "Now what?" she asked, annoyed that her pulse was beating faster.

"Do you always shop late at night?"

"I don't like crowds."

"Planning to bake more cookies?"

"No."

"Who do you make all those cookies for anyway?"

Kate finally looked back at him. His nose was red from the cold. "Why don't you think they're all for me?"

She watched his eyes. They skimmed her quickly. "Obvious reasons," he answered. "And this cart is too full of health food for a sweet tooth."

"Do you make deductions about everything?"

"I like analyzing."

"I bet you were great in geometry."

His eyebrows pinched together.

"Exceptional in logic and reasoning."

"I liked math."

"Puzzles? Taking things apart?"

"All that," he admitted. "So, who do you make the cookies for?"

"Students. Especially the younger ones. Sometimes I stop their lessons early so we'll have time to talk."

"Over cookies and milk?"

"If they're worried about their lessons, they'll tell me. If I didn't take that extra time with them, I might never learn that they're having trouble. Some children are bashful with anyone who they consider a teacher...." Her voice trailed off. Rambling. She was rambling. Why did he unsettle her so much? she wondered. "Why are you here? Are you still following me?"

"This could be a coincidental meeting."

She sent him a doubtful look. "What does your investigation entail?"

"My playing detective, getting answers to questions and, I could add, helping you shop, if you want me to."

"If I said that I prefer to do it alone, you wouldn't hear me, would you?"

"Do you have a penchant for solitude?"

She smiled weakly at the ridiculousness of his comment. "Not with you around."

With a grin, he settled back against the counter.

"But privacy is a luxury that I appreciate. I grew up with fifty-seven other children. Still, that doesn't mean I live like a hermit now."

"I didn't say that you were one. But your profession is a reclusive one, isn't it?"

"Not at all. Students come to my apartment throughout the day and evening. And I have friends."

"Male ones?"

"Occasionally," she answered cautiously. "Do I look like a woman who'd dislike male company?"

"On the contrary. You look like a woman who would have a great deal of it."

"Was that a subtle way of questioning, or was that a compliment?"

"Truth."

With two fingers on the stem, she held up a bunch of grapes, then set them down and picked up another.

He stepped closer to the counter and dangled a different bunch of grapes.

"Are you inspecting them?" she asked tersely.

"This bunch looks better than the ones you just stuffed in the plastic bag?"

"Are you an expert shopper, too?"

He grinned at her quip. "A bachelor."

"Never married?"

"I'm divorced."

"Recently."

"No."

He didn't appear the kind of man to let go of anything easily. "Are you bitter?"

Laughter crept into his voice. "Is a marriage proposal coming up?"

She shot a glare back at him.

"I liked being married," he said easily.

"So why...?"

"Just not to her."

"You say that as if she hasn't got a name."

"She has a notable one. Diane Farnson Van Hammon."

Kate released a long breath. "That sounds—"

"Her father owns several electronics corporations. Nouveau riche. The whole family is still in a period of adjustment."

Kate tilted her head curiously. "In what way?"

"They need to flaunt their status for fear someone won't notice they're wealthy."

"You're a little bitter."

"A little," he admitted.

She watched the edges of his lips tug upward in a self-deprecating grin. Kate sensed the difficult time he'd had with the failure of his marriage. She returned a hesitant smile and wandered to the celery display. "Do you cook?"

"I'm a great cook," he said, setting his bag of grapes in her shopping cart.

"And modest, too. What do you cook?"

"Anything."

She pushed her cart forward, not doubting he'd follow. "Do you have a specialty?"

"Spaghetti. What's yours?"

She lowered a jar of olives into her basket. "I rarely cook."

"When you do?"

"Pot roast."

He picked up the jar.

Kate stopped and frowned. "What are you doing?"

"Reading the label."

"They're olives."

"Green olives."

"Obviously."

"With pimentos."

"I like them that way," she said.

"From New Jersey."

"Is that important?"

"No."

"There must be a purpose to this conversation," Kate mused.

"There is."

"Are you going to tell me, or do I have to play twenty questions?"

"Look in this cart."

"Look at what?" Kate asked.

"Your groceries," he said, frowning.

Kate stared down with him.

"What people put in their grocery carts tells a lot about them."

"Always the detective?"

"Always. Like when I go shopping, I buy meat at the butcher's counter. Two of everything."

"For you and a guest."

"No, then I'd buy three. But if you'd bought two, that's what I would have deducted."

"Why for me but not for you?"

"Most women wouldn't eat two. They worry too much about their weight."

"But obviously you have a *manly* appetite."

He gave her a lopsided grin and pointed discreetly toward the other end of the aisle. "That guy bought a pound of coffee and Ding Dongs."

"For a snack," Kate said.

Brian shook his head. "For breakfast. He's wearing no wedding ring, bought a travel magazine and chose a musk deodorant."

"Maybe he was doing only his own shopping tonight."

"He's what? Thirty? If there were a wife at home, he'd have put something in that cart to tell us that there was. Something for a lady's needs or..."

"How delicately put."

"Or a box of tissue with flowers on it. But he bought a plaid box. Masculine. Everything is masculine."

Kate shook her head. "So what have you deduced from my cart?"

"That's what's bothering me. I can't figure it out. You've got lettuce, cucumbers, celery, green olives, grapes. Okay, so you're a health nut. One of those eat-your-greens-everyday people."

"I hear a question coming."

"Health nuts don't buy Popsicles, spice drops and a kid's fruit drink." His eyes skimmed the cart. "And everything is green."

"I like green food. Avocados. Spinach salads. Guacamole."

"Why?"

"It makes me think of spring. Do you always have to have a reason for everything you do?"

"That seems logical to me."

"Why did you come in here then?"

His head reared back. "Did you plan that?"

Kate smiled.

"Were you leading me on all that time to trap me?"

Saying nothing, Kate pushed her cart toward the checkout counters.

"I'll be damned," he said admiringly. "Good job."

"Thank you."

"I'll help you carry the groceries home."

Kate whirled around. He was already walking toward the magazine rack. She frowned. He wouldn't have taken no for an answer. He did exactly as he wanted, she reminded herself. He'd also left his grapes in her cart.

The sound of a cuckoo clock greeted Brian as he preceded her into the apartment. Both arms full of groceries, he waited until she flicked on a light, then ambled into the kitchen.

Sliding the bag onto the counter, he glanced around. The first time he'd entered her kitchen, he'd noticed the daisies. Less preoccupied now with getting answers to questions, he found himself experiencing the warmth of the woman through the decorations crowding the small space.

He looked up and scanned the shelf near the ceiling. Teapots of various colors and sizes adorned the shelf. "You like tea, huh?"

"Hate it."

Brian wheeled around. "But ..."

"I collect teapots."

"Why?"

"Everyone should collect something. Don't you?" she asked, digging into a grocery bag.

"No."

"How unusual."

He was unusual? Brian gave his head a shake. His gaze settled on the window. "What have you planted here?"

"Herbs."

He stared down at stems that stood no higher than newly mowed blades of grass. He heard the ticking of the clock, the rattle of paper as she folded a bag. But it was her sudden nearness, her warm exotic fragrance that enveloped him.

Standing beside him, she pointed. "This is thyme. It's a good border herb." With a fingertip, she molded dirt around the lone stem.

"Is this a hobby?"

"I suppose so. I don't really use many of the herbs for cooking. It's my little patch of ground in the world," she said lightly. "Did your family have a house?"

"I still live in it."

"Do you have a garden?"

"No green thumb."

"If I had a house, I would have one."

Well-cared-for plants hung from the ceiling, their leaves healthy. She liked nurturing, he decided. She liked springtime and fall. She liked daisies and teapots and Rachmaninoff. She was a puzzlement, he realized. "If you don't cook with herbs, then why grow them?"

She rolled her eyes. "Everything really does have to have a reason, doesn't it?"

"Yes," he said more defensively then he'd intended.

"I use them for medicine."

"Go on," he scoffed.

She faced him, raising her chin a notch. "In ancient times, herbs had strange and magical powers."

Brian raised an eyebrow skeptically.

"People thought they did," she corrected. "Chervil soaked in vinegar was used as a cure for hiccups, and sage was used as a remedy for colds. Herbs were important in Greek mythology, too. Daphne fled from Apollo by asking the gods for help. She was changed into a laurel tree."

"And being a persistent man, Apollo took to wearing laurel crowns in consolation," he said absently.

She closed the cabinet door. "You understand persistence, don't you?"

Brian leaned back against the refrigerator.

"Tenacious as a bulldog?"

"I've been told that." He shifted his stance to see into her bedroom. *Casablanca* revisited, he thought, noting the giant artificial palm tree near the bed. But stepping forward, he could see an oak headboard, lacy pillow covers and a colorful quilt. Blended in was the unexpected—bold pink-and-lavender throw pillows, an antique mirror and a circus poster of a clown.

"You're frowning again."

Brian gestured toward the poster on the bedroom wall.

"That was during my 'I'm going to run off and join the circus' phase."

"To be what?"

"A trapeze artist."

He looked back at her. "What happened?"

"I found out that I didn't like high places."

Grinning, Brian took a step toward the doorway. "And that?" He pointed at an enormous stuffed panda that held the place of honor on the overstuffed cushion of a high-back wicker chair. "From a boyfriend?"

"I won it at a fair."

He laughed, realizing he was surprised by her answer. "What's your expertise?"

"Throwing balls at milk bottles."

He strolled away from the door and into the living room. On an end table was a huge glass bottle. He wandered through the sedate living room with its overabundance of Victorian furniture to bend forward and peer at the bottle. An assortment of childish keepsakes filled it—brightly-colored marbles, a rubber spider, a pencil with a flower eraser, a plastic sheriff's badge, a skull ring. He kept turning the bottle, each time finding something different, some treasure of youth. "Is there a story for this, too?"

"Piano teachers receive unusual presents from students. I couldn't part with any of them. Finding a way to display them all was my biggest problem."

"Your students must like you."

"I hope so."

He stood still for a long moment, wanting to absorb everything. She lifted her face and smiled. He'd always been a sucker for women with dimples, but an excitement he'd never anticipated assaulted him whenever she gave him a smile. "Have dinner with me tomorrow?" he asked suddenly.

"Why? More questions?"

"Come on." He grinned, feeling young. "You know differently." Without too much thinking, he stepped closer. "Investigators don't go around asking people to dinner to question them."

"Why are you?"

"Damned if I know," he admitted softly before touching her waist. He felt her draw a quick breath. He lacked good sense if he let feelings for this woman interfere with business. But then the only business important to him since they'd met was why she'd aroused those feelings within him so quickly.

She stared up at him then, her lips parting, and desire sprang forth inside him. He'd always considered himself a man in control. So why with a mere look could this woman weaken him? "Dinner?" he whispered.

She shook her head and backed away. "I don't think that I like what you're doing to my life."

He released a semblance of a laugh. "I'm not sure I care for it, either."

"Then, don't...." she appealed.

He took a step toward her again.

"Please, leave."

Her eyes met his. He saw vulnerability. He saw her fear of being hurt and turned toward the door.

"Don't—"

He cut her words short with a whispered reply. "I'm not sure I have a choice."

As he stepped into the hall and closed the door behind him, he drew a hard breath.

Chapter Four

Kate was stunned when the deliveryman handed her a basket of kiwifruit the next morning. Then laughter tickled her throat. Hairy and ugly-looking, the exotic fruit was impossible to get in winter. Yet Brian had found them. When had any man sent her such an outlandish gift?

As her final student ambled out the door that evening, her stomach growled and complained at having to wait until eight-thirty for food. She discarded the idea of a grilled cheese sandwich or a bowl of soup. Her coat in hand, she hurried out the door and toward the stairs. All day she'd thought about Brian and the silly gift. She couldn't recall any one person ever dominating her thoughts, ever making her smile so much. The idea that he did, disturbed as much as pleased her.

No more, she chided herself as she started down the stairs. She thought back again to the audition with Breshkov.

She'd been nervous until her fingers had touched the keyboard. As she'd relaxed, she'd felt as if she could play forever for him. His presence generated the best from a performer. But when she'd finished, she'd found herself battling nervousness again.

"You will play again for me," he'd said as he'd escorted her toward the door.

She'd nearly sighed with relief. She knew that he insisted on two auditions from anyone he was seriously considering for an instructor. "I'd be honored," Kate had managed to reply.

"I will call. We will make arrangements later."

But when? Kate had wanted to ask. Instead she'd given him an agreeing nod and had said goodbye.

Then she'd seen Brian waiting for her. He annoyed and interested her more than any man she'd ever known. He also made her uneasy. He rammed his way through life. He—Kate stopped cold on the top step and stared at the man standing in front of the buzzer panel. He also didn't take no for an answer.

His finger poised, her personal Sherlock was ready to jab at a buzzer. Her buzzer, Kate reminded herself. A smile twitched at the corners of her lips as she joined him in the narrow hallway. "Didn't I say no?" she asked.

"Don't you remember what you said?"

Kate slipped an arm into her coat. "Do you always do what you want?"

"Always." He held the collar of her coat while she slid her other arm into the sleeve. "I have a suggestion."

Her blood raced, setting off nerves. He was firing up something within her that she wasn't sure she wanted flamed.

"You'll never guess what it is," he said, following her outside.

She heard laughter in his voice and felt herself melting. "Bet I will."

"We have two choices," he said as they descended the slick steps. "Dinner alone or together."

"You are pushy."

"Give me an answer."

Kate halted on the sidewalk with him. "If I say alone, then what?"

A slow smile lit his face. "Then I cross the street and walk on that side. We meet at the door of the Italian restaurant. We walk in together, but separate. And we eat at two different tables."

She couldn't help smiling. "It does sound like a silly idea."

"Glad you agree." His hand cupped her elbow. "So we'll eat together."

An insidious attraction existed. She hardly knew him. For that matter, she wasn't even sure that she liked him. They probably had nothing in common. "I bet you love country-and-western music, don't you?"

"Sorry to disappoint you. I've always liked Beethoven."

He's just saying that, she reminded herself. "Any particular pieces?" she asked, determined to call his bluff.

"His lighter compositions."

"Such as?"

"*Moonlight* Sonata." Without missing a step, he reached out and tugged her scarf up higher around her neck.

"It's one of my favorites, too," she admitted.

His knuckles brushed the underside of her jaw. "It's getting colder again."

The cloth protected her neck from the wintry wind blasting at her back, but the thoughtful gesture heated her with a warm glow. Always she'd looked out for herself. Even as a child, she'd learned not to depend on anyone else. She drew a long breath, sensing the vulnerable spot he'd touched with a simple gesture. "You know I think you're right about something."

"What's that?"

"I should keep my door locked. A woman never knows who'll stroll into her life."

"Safer."

"Yes, probably," she answered slowly.

"A little paranoia is healthy."

As they entered the restaurant, she looked up at the lights twinkling beneath the dark ceiling. "Do you really believe that?"

"Sure. It's what makes a person drive his new car like a sixteen-year-old student driver during the trip home from the showroom."

She stopped with him at the entrance to the dining room.

"It's what makes a smart woman stay off dark streets at night."

"Common sense does that."

"A little of both."

"What are you paranoid about?"

He narrowed his eyes at the hostess, a short, rotund woman, who was lumbering away instead of toward them. "That someone will try to kill me."

"Are you really?" Kate asked.

"Yeah. By starving me to death."

Kate shifted her gaze from the accordionist to Brian's plate as he pushed it away.

"You hardly dented your dinner," he said, gesturing toward her unfinished meal.

"Do you want it?"

He laughed. "No, I'm full."

"You and three other men should be. Do you always eat like that?"

He looked down at his plate. "I didn't finish the pizza."

"Not quite hungry enough?"

He smiled at her tease and dug into his pocket for his wallet. "Are you ready to go?"

"This is dutch."

"Nope."

"Are you one of those males who—"

"I seem to be," he admitted before she could finish the question. "But I let a woman pay occasionally."

"Why not now?"

He slid out of the booth. "Because I asked you out. You can pay when you ask me out."

"What if I never do that?"

"That's a chance that I'll take."

Kate heard a warning bell. The softness in his voice wrapped around her like a warm caress. She already knew that he had a relentless streak in business. Was he like that in all his pursuits? she wondered. "Do you ever take no for an answer, Fleming?"

"Another flaw," he said, not looking at all disturbed about it.

"Stubbornness."

"Do I have to admit to it?"

"No." She shook her head. "It's too obvious to deny." Kate bowed her head from the onslaught of snowflakes greeting them when they stepped outside.

"When I asked you out to dinner a few days ago, why did you refuse? You didn't have a date, did you?"

"I was invited out that night." She decided not to tell him that the invitation had come after her refusal to his. How could she explain the impact he seemed to have on her in such a short time?

"And refused him, too?"

"He wasn't my type."

"Gold chains and a sunlamp tan?"

She laughed softly. "He's quite a bit older than I."

"You're what? Twenty-seven?"

"Eight."

He stepped around her, shielding her from the northerly wind. "I'm thirty-three. Five years is a nice age difference."

"Is it?"

"Compatible."

"He's seventy."

"Who is?"

"The man who asked me out."

"Seventy!"

"He'll be married fifty years next week to a woman named Adeline, so he took lessons to play 'Sweet Adeline' to her. And he sings it, too. He wanted to take me out as a special thank-you for teaching him."

Grinning, he shook his head. "Romantic soul."

"Yes, he is."

"Are you?"

"No, I don't think so."

"I think you're wrong."

"Why do you think that?"

"You wear a perfume that smells exotic—warm—passionate. Interesting combination."

"What is?"

"A woman who wears an exotic perfume, silly sweatshirts and pink sneakers with chartreuse shoelaces."

He was trained to notice everything, she reminded herself, not willing to make more of his words than a simple observation. "I never thanked you for the basket of fruit."

"Ugly critters, aren't they?"

Kate laughed.

"But green."

"Yes, they are that. And not easy to find at this time of year."

"Not too difficult."

"For a man who never takes no for an answer?"

He grinned. "Professionally, it's a good trait."

"I'm glad you didn't take no this time," she admitted. "I've had a good time."

"Me, too." He lowered his head as a gust of wind blew snow into their faces. "This evening might be perfect if it wasn't winter, if we weren't walking in this damn snow."

"I usually like to walk in all kinds of weather." She followed the command of his hand pulling her close to sidestep a patch of ice.

"In all kinds of weather?"

"In autumn mostly. At least, years ago I did. The children's home was in the woods. Leaves turned to beautiful colors. Whenever I had a chance to go to town, I'd see people raking leaves outside their homes. The air always smelled wonderful.'' She glanced up from her boots. ''People could burn the leaves then.''

''And pollute the air. But I liked the smell, too. It usually meant that I'd finally finished raking all those leaves.''

''It's like shoveling snow. It's never ending.''

''For me, it seemed that way. My kid sister always jumped in the pile, messing it up.''

''Did you get angry?''

''Not really. But my dad would come outside and want to know what was taking me so long.''

She couldn't stop a giggle.

''I didn't think it was funny. I wanted to play football.''

''Did you tell your father why it was taking you so long?''

''He knew.''

''How did he know?''

''My sister would stand before him with that sweet, innocent face of hers, but leaves would be in her hair and all over her clothes.''

''So what happened?''

''He helped.''

''And your sister?''

''Sometimes. It depended on how hard she batted her baby blues at him.''

''How old is she?''

''Four years younger. She works at the agency with me.''

''She's a private investigator?''

''Damn good one.''

She heard pride, warmth, affection. "Would she say the same about you?"

He laughed. "Grudgingly." He opened the apartment-building door for her. "She tells me that I'm caught up in the superhero complex."

"Are you?"

"My idol is Spider-man."

Kate giggled.

"Hey, this is serious business."

"Is it?"

"Why sure. How many men do you know who can stretch from one rooftop to another?"

"Oh, yes. I see how serious that could be," she said lightly, playing along with him while she rummaged through her purse for her keys. "They're here somewhere."

"You could always borrow your neighbor's." He brushed flakes of snow from the sleeves of his coat. "It's in the mailbox. She's the one who opened the door for me that first night."

"I know." Kate frowned as she peered into her purse. "The whole idea of this second door is for security. She's probably told every deliveryman in town about the hiding place for her key."

"Don't panic. She thought I was Huntsmucker, too."

"Huntsbacker," Kate corrected. Her heart jumped as he moved near. She forced her voice to sound calmer than she felt. "Didn't you feel any surge of conscience to tell her differently?"

"No."

His breath warming her cheek, Kate bent her head and focused her attention on the key. "You're in a sneaky business."

"Think so?"

"Absolutely. You obviously take advantage of all opportunities."

Unexpectedly, he stepped back. "Not always."

Kate heard a serious note in his voice and looked back at him.

"I tried to call Dorothy Arneson again. According to a nurse at the hospital, she's in poor health. I'm going to drive there and see her."

She turned and faced him. "Why are telling me this?"

"You'd probably get more answers from her than I would. I'd like you to go with me."

Kate battled a childhood fear. She'd yearned to know the truth about her background, yet had always been frightened of it. Coming face-to-face with her past might be the only way to end all the questions that had haunted her childhood.

"Will you come with me?"

"Yes. When? Tomorrow?"

He nodded. "I'll pick you up."

"What time?"

"Probably not too early."

She took a step to the left to turn around.

He took one to the right to give her room.

"That's all right. I'm an early riser."

"I'm not," he admitted on a laugh, but she saw no humor in his face.

She felt her heart begin to thud.

"Rachmaninoff and chocolate chip cookies," he said, sounding amazed.

Kate gaped at him, thrown off balance by him again.

"You thought I was a musical illiterate, didn't you?"

"No. . . ." She paused. "But I didn't think that you knew I'd been playing—"

"Rachmaninoff's Concerto in B-flat Minor?"

"Yes."

The eyes staring at her were serious. Her heart beat faster as she sensed that he wouldn't leave abruptly this time, that he wouldn't leave without doing what he wanted to first. But she was no more ready for his kiss now than she'd been then. She placed a hand on his chest to keep some distance between them. She wouldn't let him confuse her, unsteady her this time.

As he stared at her for endless seconds, she felt herself weaken. The hand separating them no longer pushed him away. She struggled to keep control of the moment even as he brushed his lips across hers.

She tried not to think about the taste of him, but that one sense overpowered the others. A kiss was a kiss, she told herself. Some were more practiced or more passionate or more tender. She wouldn't imagine his kiss as better or sweeter or gentler than it was.

Analyzing it seemed the smartest thing to do. Her mind centered on the pressure of his arm tight against her back, the gentle strength in the hand framing her jaw and the side of her face. She smelled the scent of masculine flesh, soapy clean. And she tasted, grabbing impressions. Firmness. Heat. Seduction.

Her mouth tingled beneath the intense pressure, the demand in his kiss. His mouth conveyed a message of annoyance more than pleasure, as if he wished that he hadn't started this, hadn't wanted this. But the lips moving over hers took a deep taste as if the choice not to didn't exist.

Thoughts suddenly weren't important to her. Only feelings. Warm ones skittered through her as he kissed her thoroughly. Her mouth clung to his; her tongue answered his. She'd expected forcefulness from him. He had a hard edge, an innately dangerous quality. She had never expected the softness or gentleness of the mouth enticing hers.

A need whipped her unlike any she'd known in a long time. He probed with his tongue, seeking a deep, full taste of her mouth as if he had a right to it. Desire coiled through her. Sharp and swift and demanding. Even as she recognized the danger building, she didn't pull away, didn't stop the kiss. Her body rested against his, his angles comforting her rounder softness. Head swimming, she felt his hand roam over her. She felt desperate to absorb every sensation. She felt breathless, stunned by her own lack of resistance. She was feeling too much too fast. She roused herself to protest, though every fiber of her wanted to submit. She pulled back, insisting the moment end before she lost all will to stop him.

He trapped her to him for a moment longer. If he started again, she knew she'd slide over the edge. She expelled a long, shaky breath. In defense against her own thoughts, she drew back again. He released her, but she saw the tension in his face, felt it in her own body. The chill of winter breezed across her skin again, but the heat from his mouth still lingered on her lips. And in his eyes, she saw what she'd felt. Desire. And something more potent, she thought in a sudden panic.

Lightly, he cupped her chin and met her stare. She felt him delving inside her, searching to see beyond what was visible.

He ran a fingertip lightly across her swollen mouth then stepped back. "I'll call you before I come tomorrow."

Tell him no. Tell him that you've changed your mind, she warned herself. But her voice wouldn't work.

As if reading her thoughts, a grin tugged at the edges of his lips. "Tomorrow," he said softly. The one word sounded like a promise.

Kate said nothing, waiting until the door closed behind him. He takes my breath away, she mused. What made one person an acquaintance after years and another person a friend within hours? Whatever the mysterious quality was, she knew he wasn't a stranger any longer. Yet, he wasn't a friend, either. What was he then? Trouble, she decided.

Chapter Five

Kate flicked the far right car vent toward her. She felt on edge, not for the first time since Brian had appeared at her apartment door at daybreak. He'd greeted her as if the previous night's kiss hadn't happened, and she wished that she could forget it as easily as he had.

"You should be warmer soon."

Too warm, she thought, watching him angle both center vents in her direction. At every meeting he disarmed her. Each time he'd done something small and inconsequential, something caring that she'd never experienced before from any man. "You told me that we weren't leaving early."

"I gave the trip more thought. We might run into bad roads." He glanced at the picnic basket on the seat between them. "What's in there?"

"Coffee."

"There's a bunch of cassettes under your seat if you want some music."

Kate bent forward. She wasn't prepared for his eclectic taste: Brubeck and Beethoven. Springsteen and Schubert. Diamond and Dvořák. Because she loved music, she favored almost any kind. "Do you play a musical instrument?"

"How did you guess?"

"This looks like my collection."

Sounding like a drum roll, windshield wipers swished snowflakes to the edges of the windows.

"What do you play?"

"Saxophone."

"Do you really?"

"Why are you surprised?"

She shrugged. "I don't know." Maddeningly, she realized that he'd nudged them a little closer.

"We could try a duet sometime."

"A duet? I probably don't know the music that you know."

"You read notes," he said simply. "That's all you have to do. What about 'Blue Moon'?"

It was a favorite of hers. "Yes, I can play that."

He chuckled softly. "That's an understatement from someone who can play Rachmaninoff."

Kate slipped a cassette into the tape deck. The soft, lulling voice of Neil Diamond filled the interior of the car. Had she ever met any man who suggested playing music together? Though she knew many musicians, no one ever had. "Why did you choose a saxophone?"

"I'm not sure I would have, but a saxophone was given to me as a gift."

Kate shifted on the car seat to stare at him. "By whom?"

"My dad. He'd been a cop. When my mother died, he was left with two kids to raise by himself. He wanted more freedom in his working hours to take care of us, so he left the police force and began working as an investigator. Money was tight at first. An investigative agency has to build up a reputation and get referrals. During the first year he barely had enough money to keep the family going. But what's Christmas without a few presents?"

When he glanced at Kate, she basked in the warmth of his smile.

"He gave me a saxophone for Christmas. It had been his."

"What had you wanted?"

"A catcher's mitt."

"How old were you?"

"Nine. But I saw the look in his eyes . . ." His voice softened. "He was a big man, a tough man, and I saw tears in his eyes when he gave the gift to me. That saxophone was suddenly the most wonderful present he could have given me."

Kate turned to look out the passenger window. She'd never felt such a need to please someone else. There'd never been anyone else.

"What about you?" Brian asked, insisting on her attention. "You told me that you started taking piano lessons at seven. Did you know what you wanted to do then?"

Kate flipped back the lid of the picnic basket to pull out a coffee thermos. "Yes, in a way I did. I loved music."

"Why not performing? Why didn't you try for a position with a symphony orchestra?"

"It's too confining."

He flicked off the windshield wipers as the snow-fall decreased to flurries.

Kate looked up from pouring coffee into the thermos cup and saw his frown. "Someone telling me what music to play," she explained while offering the cup to him. "The music is mine. No one can take that from me. To make music is such a wonderful feeling. My students don't always see it that way. They don't realize it's something that they'll always have. No one can ever take it from them once they have it."

He took a sip of the coffee and handed the cup back to her. "Telltale comments."

"Why are they?"

"You don't like people telling you what to do."

"When you get to the Piedmont, you'll understand."

"Was it bad?"

"No, I didn't mean that. It wasn't unpleasant. It was very regimented, though. We had a schedule that was followed from six in the morning until three every day. And we wore lovely little uniforms. Natty white blouses with navy-blue jumpers."

Brian smiled at her.

"I was the perfect candidate for the nickname Beanpole."

"Were you called that?"

Kate returned his smile. "No, I wasn't. Everyone was nice at the home. But there were so many rules, so many things I could or couldn't do. I made a promise to myself that when I grew up, I'd live every day my way."

"And if you decide it's a day to play hooky, then what do you do?"

"Whatever."

"Come on. Like what?"

"I watch planes take off and land." She giggled at the amused look he sent her way. "And I like football games."

"Where else do you go? The symphony?"

"I've played a few times at symphony hall and the amphitheater."

"I'm impressed."

"I didn't say it to impress you. I said it to..." She paused and glanced at him.

"To what?"

Kate laughed. "To impress you."

"Do you ski?"

She hesitated, staring out the window at the falling snow. "Do you?"

Brian shook his head. "I never seem to have the time."

"Cross-country," Kate answered. Thinking about his last comment, suddenly she doubted that she'd see him after his investigation for Gertrude Stranton was finished.

"I guess I could always find a good teacher."

He made her feel too much, she realized. He made her think about a future with someone. She'd always been a loner. She'd never given too much thought to her life being different from that. She wouldn't now, either. They were like two ships that pass in the night, she told herself, grateful that someone had come up with such a reassuring cliché. Eventually he'd go his way, and she'd go hers.

But for now, he remained close.

An hour later he stood beside her as Kate looked down at the woman in the white nurse's uniform.

The woman eyed the clock, then fixed a reprimanding frown on them. "It's much too early for visiting hours. You'll have to leave."

"Is Dorothy Arneson being allowed visitors?" Kate asked.

The nurse's mouth turned down, but she pulled out a patient's chart. "I'd have to check with the doctor." She raised a sympathetic look to them. "Mrs. Arneson has been having some very difficult days lately."

Kate nodded. "We'd appreciate it if you'd check with him. We'll come back later."

"Yes, I'd be glad to."

Kate turned away from the counter. She'd expected Brian to be standing near. Instead, he was already walking down the long corridor toward the exit. Kate caught up with him at the door. "Why didn't you wait?"

Brian held the door for her. "It was hot in there."

"I don't know why you'd complain about that," she countered, stepping outside into the wind. "It felt good to..." Her words trailed off as she looked up at him. Perspiration dotted his brow. "Brian?"

"Let's get some breakfast, then head for Whispering Pines."

"Whispering Pines?"

"That's where your mother is from, isn't it?"

"Yes, according to the birth certificate."

"We'll go there. We might learn something."

Kate shook off questions she had about his reaction to the hospital. "I've already gone there."

"When?" he asked, unlocking the car door for her.

"When I left the Piedmont, I went there. There aren't any Lindstroms. And no one remembered my mother."

"We'll go again."

"I've already gone there," she insisted. She planted her feet, not responding to his hand urging her to get in the car.

"You might have missed something or someone."

"I didn't."

He blew out a long breath. "Okay. We'll make a bet."

"Why?"

"Because if we don't have a reason for going there, we're going to stand here arguing about going there until we freeze to death. So what do you want if we don't find anyone?"

It would have been simpler to agree, but Kate rebelled at his insistence. "An ice-cream cone."

"What?"

"An ice-cream cone," she repeated, enjoying the look of disbelief that had settled on his face.

"You're a little batty," he remarked lightly. "Your nose is red, you're shivering and you want an ice-cream cone?"

Kate nodded. "And what do you want?"

He held her with a look. She didn't dare let her stare waver. A challenge silently stretched between them. She was going crazy, she decided. She'd been romanced by other men—sent flowers, wined and dined, the usual male prelude to seduction. But except for a kiss, she and Brian had stood in polite opposition at almost every meeting. Yet she felt a collision instead of a retreat about to take place. Soon, she realized as she stood trapped, her back against the car.

She didn't need to hear his words to know what he'd say. She caught a faint trace of cologne. He moved so near she had to tilt back her head to maintain her steady stare. Suddenly she was willing to lose the silly bet.

Her vision blurred as he bent his head. His breath was hot on her face, a faint white mist in the air. The wind whipped around them. She hardly noticed. Lightly, he nibbled at the corner of her mouth. She didn't think to turn her face from his. He intrigued her, always doing the unexpected. She liked that quality most about him. He seemed stable and steady and yet wonderfully unpredictable. Even now, with his hand cupping the back of her neck, she anticipated the pressure of his mouth, but instead, his lips merely brushed across hers. The kiss was light, seductive, enticing—but barely a kiss.

"Much more of that..." he murmured, then caressed her lips again before he stepped back.

Repeatedly, he'd stirred conflicting feelings in her. She had admitted to an attraction, then had assured herself it could be ignored. Foolish thinking, she realized as she settled back in the car. He was so determined, so single-minded at times, so stubborn. She doubted anyone ignored him if he had decided differently.

"The wager is made, Kate." Smiling, he flicked on the ignition. "Be prepared to pay."

Obstinancy wasn't his trait alone. Kate matched his determined tone. "This is going to be a waste of time."

"We'll see."

"You never give up, do you?"

"Only when I'm forced to."

Thirty minutes later Brian slowed the car to Whispering Pines's speed limit. As the car droned at fifteen miles per hour, he mumbled, "A real boomtown."

"I tried to warn you. But you wouldn't listen. Population is four hundred. If you want to renege on the bet..."

"The bet stands."

"Whatever you say," Kate said. "Let me see. What flavor do I want?" she added in a speculating tone.

He sent her an amiable grin. "Look for the post office. You haven't won yet."

"There." She pointed.

"Where?"

"The general store."

Brian groaned.

"Lindstrom. Lindstrom?" the postal clerk repeated, narrowing his eyes.

Kate watched, fascinated at the way his Adam's apple bobbed with every word. Tall and lanky, he fit her image of what Ichabod Crane would have looked like.

"Can't say I know anyone with that name."

Kate leaned back against the counter of shelves stacked with cans, unable to resist flashing an I-told-you-so smirk at Brian.

He pretended to ignore her. "This isn't a very big town. Madeline Lindstrom," Brian persisted. "I don't see how you couldn't have known her."

"That's easy to answer." The postal clerk stretched out a lanky arm and pointed at himself. "I'm from Idaho. Haven't been here more than three years."

"Okay, thanks."

As Brian took a retreating step, Kate pushed away from the shelves to join him at the door. "Now what?" she asked, grinning.

"Don't look so smug. You still haven't won," he whispered. "Do you have a doctor in this town?" he asked, looking back at the thin man behind the counter.

"Not in Whispering Pines. Everyone goes to Doc Weatherby. He lives about twenty miles west of here."

"Has he been here for a long time?"

"Sure."

Brian squeezed Kate's shoulder. "There."

"He's been around about four years now."

Kate giggled as Brian released a long breath. He stared for a long moment at the man. "What about ranchers or farmers? There must be someone who's lived in this area for more than thirty years."

"Not that I know of."

Brian opened the door for Kate.

"Only people who've been here longer than any-one else is the Praddle family."

Brian turned back. "How long?"

"At least twenty-five years. Their daughter Eunice is the spinster schoolteacher, and she's nearly thirty."

Kate groaned.

"Could you give me directions to their place?" Brian asked, ignoring Kate.

With directions to the Praddles's home, he ushered Kate out of the store before she tongue-lashed the un-suspecting mail clerk.

"'Spinster schoolteacher'!" Kate fumed as they drove out of town. "I can't believe he said that about a woman who's not even thirty yet."

"Yeah," Brian soothed, keeping his eyes on the road. "Such archaic thinking. Look for a fork in the road."

"I'm not sure I'd recognize one. Some of these so-called roads look like cattle paths."

"Anything that resembles one, okay?" He hunched forward and peered at a turnoff. "That must be it."

Mrs. Praddle greeted them with small-town neighborliness. A rotund woman with a bright grin, she wiped her hands on the front of her bib apron and invited them in without hesitation. "I knew Madeline," she informed them quickly.

Brian leaned back in the kitchen chair. He loved winning at anything—softball games, checkers, marksmanship contests and especially nonsensical little wagers. Briefly, his eyes met Kate's. He couldn't keep himself from grinning at her.

"You're a relative, aren't you?" the woman asked, bending slightly and peering at Kate. "You look like her. She was a pretty thing. Her pa ran a feed store for a while, but business got slow and he sold it."

"Did they live near here?" Brian asked, settling down to business again.

"About five miles from here. They had a farm. He tried working it, but he never really made a success of it. His land wasn't very good," she added. "Madeline wasn't too happy living way out here. She'd gotten used to living in the town. Soon as she could, she took off."

Brian leaned forward, resting his forearms on his thighs. "Took off?"

"She went to Denver. She took some typing in high school and went there for a job. She was a nice girl." Mrs. Praddle bobbed her head. "But she had a lot of high-falutin' ideas for a farm girl. She kept saying she was going to have everything she'd always wanted."

Brian cast a look at Kate. Her face was composed, but he saw sadness in her eyes. It knocked the wind from him. And he sensed the more digging he did, the more he'd see that same look in her eyes. In that second, he realized that he wanted to protect her.

"After she left," Kate asked, "did you ever see her again?"

"Oh, sure," the woman said, nodding exaggeratingly. "About five years later, she came back home."

"Here?" Brian questioned.

"That's right. We were real surprised to see her again. Never thought she'd come back. Her ma was always telling us how well she was doing and about all the friends she had in Denver and all the important people she met at the law firm where she worked. So when she came back, we thought it was kind of funny." She clucked her tongue. "But sometimes things don't work out the way people think they will."

Brian forced himself to ask the next question. "Do you know why she came back?"

"She was going to have a baby. No husband. She had nowhere else to go. So she came home to ma and pa. Then things just got worse."

Kate stood and strolled to the sink. "In what way?"

"She was so happy after she had her baby. Pretty like Madeline. But the baby was sickly. I don't remember exactly what was wrong with her. But Madeline thought it was just a cold. Then it got worse, so she took the baby to the doctor. She was just so upset when the baby had to go in the hospital. But that saved the little one."

Brian couldn't stand the distance between him and Kate. Tense, she stood with her back ramrod straight, as if ready to face a firing squad. He rose and circled the table to stand beside her.

"The car accident took all of them. The baby was saved because she was in the hospital. Everyone around here felt real bad."

Brian slipped an arm around Kate's shoulders. He'd offered the most natural response without knowing if she'd accept it. Her body leaned into his, but he sensed no weakness. He saw strength as she raised her chin a notch.

"There wasn't anyone to take the child, so she was placed in the custody of a state agency."

"A *state* agency?" Brian queried.

"Yes, that's right."

"Wrong," Brian said softly when they were back in the car. Along the tree-lined highway, branches drooped beneath the heavy burden of snow. "It's all wrong, Kate. Your mother couldn't have left the kind of inheritance that would be large enough for you to be transferred to a private children's home."

"Or for me to pursue music."

"Or that," he said, stopping the car at the fork in the road. "She was a small-town girl. She came from a hardworking farmer's family. There's no way that kind of money could have existed."

"So who did provide it?"

He heard the cool, controlled sound in her voice. "I'll have to find out. Kate..."

She shook her head at his softening tone. "Don't! Don't feel sorry for me. I don't really feel anything, Brian. It's as if everything we're learning is being said about someone else—not me. None of it has ever been a part of my life."

"Are you afraid to find out the rest?"

"I'd be lying if I said I wasn't. But then I really don't have a choice anymore. I have to know now. I need to know the name of the man who wasn't there for her." *For me.*

Chapter Six

Kate sat beside the hospital bed and touched the woman's hand. It was cold and gray.

"I'm glad you came, Katherine. I wanted to talk to you, tell you that I'm—I'm sorry."

Dorothy Arneson offered Kate a soft smile. It took effort, Brian noted.

Gently Kate squeezed her hand. "Please, don't worry yourself."

Brian stepped back to give them privacy. He felt a choking sensation just being in the sterile room, inhaling the scent that symbolized disease and illness to him. He shook his head, pushing aside his own feelings, and settled his hips on the wide window ledge.

"You were lied to, Katherine," the woman said in a shaky, staccato manner. "I have no real excuse for doing it. I can only tell the truth now and hope you'll forgive me and others."

Brian stared at Kate's back. So slender, so straight, as if she were bracing herself for a whirlwind of some kind.

"I was called and told to have you transferred from a state agency to Piedmont. I never believed the story I was told."

"What story?" Kate asked, leaning forward as if needing to hear the woman better.

"That your mother had left an inheritance. It was so large. And I checked immediately. She was from a family that wouldn't have had such money." A pained expression settled on her face. "But I was told that there would be enough money to give you whatever you needed until you were eighteen."

"How did you get this money?"

"Just as I told you when you were younger. I repeated the lie just as I had heard it. I was afraid not to for fear I'd reveal too much. The man said that he was your mother's lawyer, that he'd established an account for you for your support. An inheritance, he'd insisted." The old woman looked away for a second. When her eyes came back to Kate, they were glazed with moisture. "I was offered money, a sizable contribution for the home. It was needed so much, Katherine. I knew that so many children would benefit from that money," she said appealingly. "I couldn't not take it."

Emotion edged Kate's voice. "What did you get the money for?" she asked.

"A promise. A promise not to tell anyone."

"Tell anyone what?"

"I knew he was lying to me. I insisted on knowing the truth. He refused. He said that he couldn't explain the true circumstances to me. But the money for the home was mine if I promised not to tell anyone about him or where the money came from.''

Kate straightened.

''Please, please, don't think too badly of me. I wanted to tell you the truth but...'' Shakily, the old woman lifted her head from the pillow. ''Oh, Katherine, I'm so sorry.''

''It's all right,'' Kate assured her. ''It's all right,'' she repeated, enclosing the woman's hands with her own. ''Please tell me who came to you.'' Her voice was low but steady. ''Who was the man?''

''Douglas Stranton.''

Brian walked beside Kate down the hallway toward the hospital exit. He'd said nothing to her since they'd arrived at the hospital, she realized. She looked up at him, expecting to see an expression marked with professional cynicism or a frown filled with sympathy. His face was bathed in perspiration. ''What's wrong?'' she asked. ''Are you ill?''

He shook his head. ''Are you okay?''

She heard his concern, his willingness to comfort. ''I'm fine, really. But you're not.''

''I will be in a minute.'' He stepped forward and flung open the hospital door.

As they stepped outside, the panicked look she'd seen disappeared from his face. ''Was it being in the hospital that bothered you?''

''Forget it,'' he insisted sharply.

Kate nodded.

''I'm sorry. You're probably going through a dozen emotions, and I'm—I'm acting like a real ass.''

Kate responded to his weak smile. "I'm really not," she said. "I feel nothing. I thought I would, but I don't."

"No anger?"

She released a mirthless sound that vaguely resembled a laugh. "I'd lie if I said that I don't feel any anger."

"No hurt?"

Kate met his eyes. He was pushing her, prodding her to at least feel something. And he was offering her comfort if she needed it. "Yes, hurt." She swallowed hard. "Why did he walk away from me? Why didn't he—" She stopped, the words catching in her throat so suddenly that she was rocked by her own reaction. She turned her back to Brian as she struggled with the wrenching words that had haunted her repeatedly since she'd left Dorothy Arneson's hospital room.

"Kate."

So soft, his voice was as soft as a whisper. She felt his hands on her shoulders and shook her head, wanting to avoid the moment. Gently, persuasively, he turned her around to face him. Kate drew a quick breath. She felt moisture on her cheeks. She hadn't expected tears. She hated them. Desperately she wanted to feel nothing. But one question nagged at her, one question compressed her chest and tightened her throat with a pain unlike any she'd ever known. "Why didn't he want me?"

Brian pulled her against him. She felt the strength of his body supporting her, the heat of him warming her, his soothing touch on her hair as his fingers tenderly stroked the back of her head. She couldn't resist the comfort of another's arms at a moment when she felt so totally alone.

He remained quiet, but with a simple gesture he told her that she wasn't alone. Tears flowed as she came face-to-face with the years of rejection, of abandonment. And through it all, Brian said nothing. He simply held her.

Brian tried to rationalize his feelings for her. Attraction, enjoyment, desire. Yes, and something else. As he turned the car onto the road toward Denver, he avoided naming that one emotion, aware of what it might mean to both of them. "I'll check some other things when we get back."

"Like what?"

She still sounded shaky. She still looked pale, he thought. "Records. Don't jump to conclusions, Kate. All you have is Dorothy Arneson's story. That's not proof."

"Are you talking about proof that my mother knew Douglas Stranton?"

He nodded.

"Are you saying that she might have lied? Why would she lie now? The poor woman was trying to ease her conscience. You could see that, couldn't you?"

"You're probably right, but—"

"Don't jump to conclusions," she finished for him. At his nod, she commented, "We have both done that enough already, haven't we?"

His eyes met hers. He saw strength. For such a delicate-looking woman, she possessed the inner strength to stand alone, to keep going no matter what came her way. He'd seen that in her immediate acceptance of Dorothy Arneson's remorse. He'd seen that same spirit when she'd finished crying. She'd smiled. No matter how many cool looks she sent his way from now on, he'd never forget the smile she'd managed in the midst of deep personal pain.

"What kind of records will you check?"

"Social Security records. We need to know where your mother worked while she lived in Denver."

"Are you going to make a report to Gertrude Stranton?"

"She's the one who hired me."

"I expect nothing from her."

Brian shot a look at her.

"I know who I am. I'm Katherine Lindstrom. I'm satisfied with my life. I don't need anything from them. Ever," she insisted firmly. "You tell her that."

"You don't realize what you're saying."

"Brian, I know what I'm saying."

"You could be Katherine Stranton."

Kate glanced at her watch. "I could be late for one of my students' lessons."

He sensed she was choosing a way to dodge their discussion, but Brian saw no point in pursuing it. That she might be Katherine Stranton seemed quite possible. At the moment, though, she was the woman whom he'd met days ago, pushing cookies off a baking sheet, playing Rachmaninoff and worrying about a father's insensitivity to his child's agony over piano lessons.

"And like you," she said after a moment, "I do like to eat. To do that, I have to earn a living. Did you ever want to do anything but snoop?"

Brian's head fell back with laughter.

"You do snoop."

He worked hard to stop laughing. "Okay, I snoop. And, no, I never doubted what I'd eventually do."

"Because your father had the agency?"

"I suppose so. I took criminal science in college, wavering between joining the police department or eventually going for a law degree or something with my dad."

"What determined your choice?"

He noticed that she'd shifted, relaxing and moving closer to him. "I got married. I couldn't afford to spend years reading law books, and I was too much of a nonconformist to follow the rigidness of the police department. When I realized that Serpico probably began his career in a blue uniform, standing in the middle of a street, directing traffic and looking like a flapping duck, I knew where I belonged."

"You say that so easily."

"What?"

"'I knew where I belonged.'"

Despite his resolve to keep his distance, he ached for her. "I guess that I did. My dad gave that to us. He was a wonderful man. It hit me hard when he died."

Her quietness forced him to continue.

"He taught me so many things. The most important one was that only a fool takes unnecessary risks. And then he forgot his own advice."

"What happened?"

"Life is filled with irony. He'd been in the business twenty-one years. He was a careful, thorough investigator. He walked into a grocery store where some punk, high on drugs, was holding customers at gunpoint. He was too smart to play hero just for the sake of doing it. But from what we learned, one of the customers made a quick move, and the gunman reeled around. My dad jumped in. He took the bullet that would have hit a pregnant woman." Brian shook his head, remembering the days following his father's death as if they were lined up before him on flash cards.

"How long ago did it happen?"

"Three years ago. Every year an award is handed out in his name to an investigator who's performed some heroic deed. He'd have liked that," Brian said, smiling.

"Is there just your sister now?"

"A cast of thousands if you count cousins. My dad came from a big family. Seven sisters and a brother. My grandfather was a cop, too. A hard-line, follow-the-rules cop. My dad always had a soft spot. He was one of the best," he said simply. "Then there was his younger brother." Brian rocked his hand. "He was as shady as my dad was lawful. I saw him destroy himself wanting things. He needed the best car, the best clothes. Money became his food of life. And he'd do anything to get it."

"Anything?"

"My grandfather was at the police station the night my uncle was arrested." He glanced at her. "A cop who believed everything was black or white watched his son getting booked."

"Do you believe in bending rules?"

"Sometimes." He smiled. "Sometimes we just can't control everything. We don't always have choices." He hadn't had any about her. He wondered if she was aware of the rightness between them. Yet, he knew as right as everything seemed, something was wrong. For days he'd believed his feelings had stirred from his wanting something untouchable—her. But was it simply desire? He doubted that. He wasn't a stranger to passion. He understood wanting a woman. So why did he feel a need to be with her? Why did he need to protect, to comfort her? Need and want weren't the same thing, he warned himself. One carried a stronger commitment. There was the problem. He could make a commitment to Kate Lindstrom. But what about Katherine Stranton?

Kate stared out the window at the passing scenery. She'd heard such affection, such love when he'd talked about his family. He was like his father, she decided. Strong and masculine, yet compassionate and sensitive. A comfortableness existed between them in an amazingly short amount of time. Was that because he offered what she'd needed in life? He'd cared about her. He didn't need to say the words. She felt the caring. It touched her deeply. It scared her—confused her. But then, he'd confused her from the moment he'd strolled into her apartment.

"We have to make a stop in the next town."

Kate shifted on the car seat as he began slowing his speed. "This is turning into perfect weather for penguins," she murmured. When he eased into a parking space, she glanced around. The small town's main street was deserted and carpeted with a new layer of snow. Kate looked around her for a gas station, puzzled that he hadn't stopped at one. When he opened the door for her, she was tempted not to get out of the warm car.

"Come on," he urged.

Reluctantly joining him on the sidewalk, she hunched her shoulders. The wind whipped at her neck and blasted snow flurries into her face.

"What flavor?"

"Fl—fl . . ."

Grinning, he closed his fingers around her arm. "You wanted an ice-cream cone."

Kate balked. "I lost the bet."

"I'm a gracious winner."

"You're sadistic," she said, shivering.

"Don't ask for what you don't want."

"I'll remember that," she returned on a laugh.

"What flavor?"

"Pistachio. Double scoop."

An hour later he braked the car at the curb in front of her apartment building. Kate shoved back the sleeve of her coat and glanced at her wristwatch. "I have ten minutes to spare. And I'm grateful. Lisa Manington's mother is a tyrant about punctuality."

"Isn't she, though?"

Kate frowned. "How would you know?"

"I know Estelle Manington."

"Did you do some work for her?"

"No, I was late for a dinner party at her house. I thought I was going to be drawn and quartered by the butler."

Kate smiled. "What did you do about it?"

"Apologized. Estelle was civil. My father-in-law was less forgiving."

Brian switched off the ignition and shoved open the car door. He hadn't thought about those days in years. At times he'd felt as if he'd never been married. Now, all of a sudden, memories about his life with Diane kept haunting him. Some of them were ones he'd have liked to forget forever.

* * *

"Can I ask you something?" Kate asked as they fought their way against the wind to cross the icy sidewalk.

"Since I've been poking my nose in your business, that seems fair."

Kate responded to his grin before asking, "What happened at the hospital?"

He shrugged. "Some people have trouble with heights. I have trouble with hospitals."

"A phobia?" She gave him a doubting look. "You don't appear to be the kind of man who gives in to phobias."

"What gives you that impression?"

"People with phobias don't think about how great it would be to stretch across rooftops like Spider-man."

Brian smiled. "I spent too many hours in them—twice."

"Can you talk about it?"

"It just bothers me to be there. When I was a kid, I visited the hospital for months before my mother died. After my father was shot, I rushed to the hospital. I reached the emergency room door as he died."

"Why did you go to see Dorothy Arneson at the hospital if you felt that way?"

Brian jammed a hand into his coat pocket. "I had to talk to her. So I had to go."

He spoke the obvious truth, but she knew differently. She had needed him. Had he expected that? How could he? Even she'd been unprepared for such a need. Yet, when it had occurred, she'd been grateful that she hadn't been alone. "Thank you," she said at the door.

"For the ice-cream cone?"

She faced him in the narrow hallway. "For being at the hospital—for being there for me."

"Anytime."

His eyes met hers with a soft, affectionate look. It disturbed her more than the one filled with desire that she'd repeatedly seen at almost every encounter. "I have to go up. Lisa and Estelle and all that."

His hands touched her shoulders. Kate stood still, expecting him to collect on the wager, wanting him to. She nearly closed her eyes in anticipation. But seconds passed, and the distance remained between them. Feeling foolish, she raised her face. She saw his frown, his eyes looking past her.

"What do you see?" Kate turned her head and craned her neck to look down the main-floor hallway.

"Stay here," he ordered before brushing past her.

"Brian?"

"Stay," he yelled in a whisper.

Kate watched him rush down the hallway. She started to follow him, then reconsidered. Letting common sense lead her, she ran up the stairs toward her apartment. She didn't view him as an alarmist. Breathing heavily, she placed a foot on the top step, wondering how long it would take to open her door and call the police emergency number.

She heard the scuffling on the stairs before she saw Brian hovering over someone threateningly. His back to her, he was poised with a raised fist.

As Kate rushed forward, Liz scurried down the hall from her apartment.

"What happened?" Liz yelled.

Kate shook her head. "I don't know." They reached Brian at the same moment.

Stepping back, he revealed a blustery faced, balding man.

Free from Brian's grasp, the man flared, "Who the hell are you? Who is this guy?" He waved an arm in Brian's direction, but glared at Liz. "Is this the new guy?"

"What *new* guy?" Liz screamed back.

Brian turned a puzzled look on Kate. She grabbed his arm and pulled him back to remove him from the line of verbal fire. "That's Harry," she said low. "Liz's husband."

Brian grimaced. "Hey, I'm sorry," he said quickly. "I saw you sneaking around and I . . ."

Harry's thick black eyebrows bunched together as he scowled at him. "Who is he?" he demanded from Liz.

"It's none of your business who he is, Harry. You moved out of the apartment. You wanted space."

"Space doesn't mean—this." Angrily he thrust his arm in a sharp jabbing motion toward Brian.

Liz stepped away from him and took off back down the hall. "When you figure out what it does mean," she yelled back, "let me know."

A door slammed hard behind her.

Brian turned to Harry and raised his hands in an apologetic palms-up gesture. "Sorry."

The anger gone from his face, Harry nodded, not answering. Stoop shouldered, he shuffled down the hallway, shaking his head and muttering to himself.

"They're a real pair," Kate said. "Combustible."

"It works for some."

"It's not working for them," Kate replied as they wandered toward her door.

She fumbled with the keys, her attention shifting to his close proximity as he set a hand against the door frame. Madness, she decided, facing him. It was madness not to make a quick departure. But she'd worry about sanity later. At the moment she seemed unable to think about anything but the pleasure she knew she'd find in his kisses. "The wager? Right?"

He brushed her cheek with the back of his hand. Her softness soothed him. Not just the softness of her flesh, but the softness and vulnerability within her that had reached out and touched him, made him care. He took a deep breath and inhaled her scent. He wanted to crush her to him and not let her go. He could without resistance. He sensed that, because of a silly wager, she'd put up no barriers this time. But winning didn't always mean satisfaction. What was the point if she didn't feel the same unbearable need that he did? "To hell with the wager," he said in a low voice.

"You don't plan to collect?"

"Should I?"

She murmured something against his lips, something that resembled a moan. He didn't need words. He needed a message of her mouth on his. As her arms curled around his neck and he tasted the sweetness of her lips, he began to relax. She had to deepen the kiss this time. Only that would make the moment right.

Her lips caressed his for several seconds. Still he waited and he ached. His mouth heated beneath the warmth of hers. The earth didn't move, he told himself. But he felt the tremor of an explosion rocking him. He couldn't avoid it. He couldn't wait for her hunger when he was already starving. He pressed himself closer to her, urging her to know the same consuming fire that was running rampant through him. As her mouth twisted against his, patience fled.

Behind her, the door swung open as if inviting them in. Somehow they no longer stood in the hall. He couldn't recall moving inside. He couldn't think about anything but the mouth as hungry as his own, the soft body straining against his.

Her soft whimper echoed the silent moan in his mind as he slid his hand beneath her coat. Soft. She was so damn soft, he thought, feeling an obsession consuming him. He wanted to lose himself in the moment. He closed his eyes, memorizing her sharp angles, her curves.

She fueled him, her hands roaming down and then up his back, caressing his neck and his face and entwining in the hair at the nape of his neck. A desperation engulfed him as he felt a willingness in the lips clinging to his and her welcome to his tongue's invasion.

He'd known she'd feel this way. Slim and warm. He breathed in the scent of her. He captured her breaths inside his mouth as desire curled around him. He felt driven to taste more of her, all of her. He couldn't let her go, not now—not ever. Need throbbed through him, insisting on him not leaving until he shared what had been only a fantasy since they'd met.

When she turned her mouth from his, he recaptured it. He devoured with a wildness, a greed that he'd never known before. Her heart pounded beneath his palm like a drum. It beat out an urgent message. He could have her now. Her passion was blending with his. Yet he felt her pushing away again. And again, she tore her mouth from his.

"Oh, Brian." His name sounded ragged on her lips.

Sanity still threatened to rule his actions. He wanted to silence her. The moment didn't have to end like this, he told himself, but another sound, the unmistakable nagging of the downstairs buzzer echoed up the staircase.

"Estelle," Kate managed on a breathless tone.

He pulled back, breathing heavily, aware then that he'd reached beneath her blouse, that only flimsy silk shielded the soft flesh of her breast from the touch of his fingers.

"Oh, Brian, I didn't mean for that to happen," she whispered on a shaky note.

He tempted himself with one more quick taste of her swollen mouth. "I did. I want you," he said huskily. As she shook her head, a strand of hair enticed him. He coiled it around his finger. Silk. She was like silk. Everywhere. "Tell me." He pressed forward, forcing her back against the door frame, trapping her. "Tell me your mouth lied to me during that kiss?" Slowly he ran a fingertip across her parted lips. He felt the heat of her breath, he felt her sigh. "I know differently. Say you don't want me," he whispered against the curve of her jaw. "Say it. And I won't come back."

She shook her head but said nothing.

Beneath his palm, her cheek was warm. He knew her wariness, understood it somewhat. "I won't hurt you. I won't," he murmured against her lips.

The buzzer droned continuously.

"Oh, damn." Aching, he stepped back. "I'll let her in," he said, turning away, fighting the longing that made him want to whip around and close the door behind them. "I'll call you. Tomorrow."

"Brian."

He heard her call out, but he kept walking. Any denial she gave him would fall on deaf ears. She'd played a different melody to him minutes before. A melody that he'd never forget.

Chapter Seven

Kate plugged in the coffee brewer and stared out the kitchen window at a pewter-colored morning sky. She'd done her best to avoid thinking about Brian ever since she'd awakened. All of ten minutes, she thought disgustedly. She couldn't forget those moments at the door, the desire that had stirred with a trembling quickness. Passion could be ignored or appeased. But what was she to do about the way he made her feel? How did she ignore that?

Yawning, she contemplated going back to bed for another half hour. A knock on the door pushed the idea aside.

"Katie?"

On another yawn, Kate shuffled to the door and opened it. "Liz, what are you doing here so early? It's—" Kate paused and glanced at her wristwatch "—it's not even six-thirty."

"Do I look as if I've been out already?" Liz questioned, looking down at her chenille robe.

Kate smiled. "No. Come on in."

"Your buzzer isn't working again," she announced, following Kate into the kitchen.

"Sure it is."

"Can't be."

Kate looked up from pouring coffee into a cup for her.

"This," Liz announced, producing a green teapot from behind her back, "was delivered for you."

"This morning?" Kate asked, staring at the hand-painted Oriental teapot and the white daisies arranged inside it.

Liz grinned, nodding. "The deliveryman said he leaned on your buzzer, but got no answer."

Kate stepped closer, nodding.

"No card. I looked," Liz admitted unabashedly.

Kate trembled. All the power of reason couldn't overshadow the pleasure coursing through her.

"No card, Katie. Who sent it?"

Kate smiled and took the teapot from her. "Sam Spade."

"I see."

"You see nothing," Kate countered, looking back over her shoulder at her friend.

"He isn't investigating you anymore?"

"No, he isn't." She set a coffee cup on the table. "Have a seat."

"Will you tell me everything?"

"Will you?"

Liz tipped her head questioningly.

"What is going on with you and Harry?"

A hint of a smile tugged the edges of Liz's lips. "I've never seen Harry jealous before."

"Liz, why don't you sit down and talk to him?"

"We'd only end up arguing again."

"It's obvious that he's sorry."

"I don't want to be hurt again."

Kate touched her hand. "No, I wouldn't want to be, either, but you're miserable without him, aren't you? Why are you fighting yourself...?" Her voice trailed off as she considered her own words. She gave her head a quick mental shake to ignore the direction of her own thoughts.

"Katie?"

"What?"

"I asked you about your private eye. What is going on between you and Mr. Nine?"

"Lust."

Liz giggled. "You have such a way of simplifying things. But are you sure that's all it is?"

"Why would you question that?"

Liz gestured toward the teapot. "That."

"It's beautiful, isn't it?"

"Unusual gift."

"Oh, Liz, come on. You've had men send you presents. What did they usually want from you?"

"Harry sent me presents before we were married."

"You can't generalize. Just because the man you fell in love with sent you presents doesn't mean every man who sends you presents is in love with you."

"No." Liz peered over the top of the cup at her. "But the kind of present is what really matters. What have you gotten from other men?"

"Candy. Flowers. Perfume."

"Harry sent me a ceramic dove. The dove means 'beloved.'"

The wistful sound in Liz's voice carried an anguished message. Look where love took people, Kate reminded herself.

"And you haven't been sent anything ordinary, either, like flowers or—"

"There are daisies in that teapot."

"There are daisies everywhere in this kitchen, Katie."

"But—"

"And teapots everywhere."

Kate drew a deep breath. "What are you trying to say?"

"He cares. He isn't just trying to please you. He's trying to touch you."

Kate looked away. "I don't want to fall in love with him."

Liz stared silently at her.

"And I don't want him to fall in love with me."

Liz shook her head slowly. "Oh, Katie, I think you're too late to wish for that."

Brian climbed the stairs toward his office and wondered when he had tossed away his original plan to keep some distance between Katherine Lindstrom and himself? And what did it matter, anyway? It had been a dumb plan.

No, it hadn't been, he argued with himself. She could be part of a family that was worth millions. She could be headed toward a life-style that he already knew he hated. He should have accepted her initial reluctance to him. He'd felt it often enough, as if she sensed some underlying problem. He hadn't meant to push so hard, so insistently into her life.

But, of course, he had. He couldn't say when it had happened. But at some moment, love had crept in on him. The realization stunned him. Attraction had made him steamroll his way into her life, but he knew now that he'd no longer be satisfied with only the magic of passion. He wanted memories of her.

He wanted years of memories. And he doubted that she was ready to accept the idea. Too much was happening in her life. Yet he couldn't back off. Not now. He couldn't take the chance of losing. He wouldn't lose her, he decided as he entered his office.

"Morning," he greeted casually.

His sister glared back at him.

Brian frowned in puzzlement. "How can you start a day looking so crabby?"

"You have a friend waiting for you," Sabrina said not too sweetly.

Tom stepped forward and grinned. "Your sister isn't happy to see me."

Brian sighed heavily, but said nothing about his sister's none-too-subtle dislike for his friend. "What can I do for you?" he asked, settling his hips on the edge of the desk.

"He needs help for the annual banquet," Sabrina piped in.

"Who's getting the award this year?" Brian asked. He nodded agreeably as Tom named a private investigator who'd spent several months in the hospital after a heroic act.

"And Uncle Charley has roped me into several committees." Tom glanced at Sabrina. "You're expected to present the Thomas Fleming Award to the winner this year, as usual.''

''I wouldn't miss the banquet,'' Sabrina assured him.

''And you, Brian—''

Brian closed one eye. ''Here it comes. What committee have you volunteered me for?''

''Entertainment.''

Sabrina released a laugh that sounded like a snort.

Brian pointed a finger at her. ''Watch it. I play a jazzy sax.''

''No!'' Tom responded quickly. ''We don't want you to play the sax.''

''I should be crushed.''

Tom laughed. ''You wouldn't do that to us.''

''You have no ear for talent,'' Brian responded, grinning. ''So what do you want?''

''We want you to round up some musicians.''

''I have some connections.''

''A music teacher?'' Sabrina asked.

''Your problem hasn't gone away?'' Tom said more than asked. ''Dangerous.''

To my heart, Brian mused. ''That's the name of this game, isn't it?''

''If it's a game.''

Far from it, Brian reflected quietly.

Kate watched her clothes tumble in the dryer and listened to the muffled sounds of an afternoon soap opera coming through the basement vent.

What if Liz was right? What if Brian was falling in love with her? She was accustomed to being alone in life. She'd always been her own person, made her own decisions. She hadn't looked for anything but her career. So many of the girls she'd known at the children's home had yearned for a family life. Kate had resigned herself to never having it. If Dorothy Arneson hadn't been lying, then . . . Kate shook her head, refusing to think about the Strantons.

Restlessly she strolled to the folding counter. Brian was proving enough of a complication. Something more complex than desire kept drawing them closer. Something was happening for the first time in her life, Kate realized, and it scared the daylights out of her. Despite what she'd said to Liz, she knew that she was falling in love.

"You're not an easy woman to find, Kate."

Startled, she jumped and whirled around. "Brian." She pressed a hand to her chest. "Will you stop sneaking around." She worked hard not to be affected by his grin, but she felt suddenly warm.

"I did some checking this afternoon."

As he moved to stand beside her, Kate looked up.

He was looking down. A finger under each strap, he slowly lifted a pink silk teddy into the air.

Kate snatched it from him. "What did you find out?"

He grinned roguishly. "More than I expected to. Ethel Haggerty wore cotton undies and support hose."

"Who is Ethel Haggerty?"

"My Aunt Ethel, the piano teacher." He brushed his fingertips over a peach-colored nightgown. "You don't."

Kate looked sideways at him. "How do you know what your aunt wore?"

"She lived next door. She hung her clothes on a line. I used to sit in my bedroom. It was on the second floor, and I'd shoot spitballs through a straw at her undies.''

Kate stifled a grin as she stacked a pillowcase on top of another.

"Kate, those dimples give you away every time. Even when you don't want to smile, they make cute little creases in your cheeks.''

She reached into the basket to dodge his touch. She already knew the danger in it. "Maybe I enjoy doing laundry.''

"Do you?''

"I hate it.''

He chuckled and sat back on the table, shifting to stare at her. "It's not so bad.'' He reached into her basket and pulled out a towel.

"There has to be a reason for everything you do. You told me that.'' She looked up at the ceiling with its network of pipes. "So that means you've come up with some—some insane reason for liking it.''

"We're alone, aren't we?''

She heard the tenseness in his voice. She felt her heart pound harder. Self-preservation was her first thought. She didn't want to get hurt. She kept her eyes downward. She didn't need to look at him to remember the warmth and the passion she'd already seen in his gaze. "When you were married, did you like doing the laundry with your wife?''

He looked away for a second. "We never did it together.''

"She did it?''

"No, Diane would never do the laundry. It was one of those jobs that she considered too plebian for her.''

"Who did it?''

"The maid.''

Kate shot a look at him. "You had a maid?"

"She had a maid."

Kate's sixth sense told her to back off from asking too many questions. A hint of discomfort in his voice warned her to change the subject. "Are you going to keep me in suspense or tell me why you're here?" She laughed. "Other than to help me with my laundry," she added, noting that he'd folded several towels while they'd talked.

The soft, glazed look lifted from his eyes. "I found out where your mother worked in Denver."

"A law firm." She shrugged. "So? We knew that."

"Wendell and Stranton and Associates."

Kate let a dish towel slip from her fingers. "Who did my mother work for there?"

"I don't know yet." He touched the teddy again. "I have to find someone cooperative who's been working there for a long time." He looked at her then. "Students tonight?"

"No," Kate answered, guessing where the conversation was going. "A free evening to myself."

"Why be alone when you could be with someone?"

"Someone in particular?"

"Isn't it obvious." He set the folded garments in her basket. "Here." He grabbed her hand.

Kate felt him place a piece of paper on her palm. "What's this?"

He closed her fingers over it.

Quickly Kate uncurled them.

"It's paper," he said as he turned away.

"I can see it's paper. But what is it?" She unfolded the small sheet of paper.

"An address." Brian started up the basement stairs.

"What?"

He ducked and looked down at her. "My address. Dinner will be ready at seven."

He wasn't sure she'd come for dinner. He considered the possibility while he set the table and prepared the meal. And he considered what was happening to him. He'd dated regularly since his divorce, but not seriously. Dating got harder as a man got older. Gone were the adolescent thrills. He'd long passed the time of wooing some girl to a drive-in or agreeing to a casualness that included fitting others into his life. His needs were greater, stronger. He wanted someone to share his life with, have a family with. He wanted to get married again, but he wasn't willing to plunge back into such a permanent arrangement without being sure about the other person. Being burned once did make a person wary of the fire. And damn, there was enough heat between him and Kate to start an inferno. Every time he saw her, it smoldered as if waiting for the right moment to flare.

He felt it immediately when he opened the door and saw her standing before him, smiling. It was a matter of time. Trust. Love. When they all came together, everything would click as if they'd been made for each other.

Kate accepted a drink and scanned the living room. It was masculine. The smells of leather and wood permeated the air. Everything was neat and in place, and she felt a charge of pleasure that he'd spruced up the house just for her. Circling the room, she noticed a stained, wrinkled letter on the end table. "Did the mail carrier drop that in the mud and snow?"

"No. I had to hunt for that letter."

"Where did you get it from?"

"A garbage can."

She pointed a finger at the envelope. "What are the stains on it from?"

"The letter was jammed between a discarded catsup bottle and a jar of moldy jelly."

She stepped close. "Ooh, that stinks." She wrinkled her nose. "For an investigation?"

"It's not my kind of case. Divorce. A letter to the husband," he added as explanation.

"From a lady friend."

"More that a lady friend. She's his wife."

"Who's his wife?"

"The so-called girlfriend."

"Two wives?"

"That's what the letter proved."

She followed him to the kitchen. A half-finished jigsaw puzzle was strewn across the kitchen table. The spicy scents of oregano, garlic and onions hung in the air. When he lifted the lid of a pot to stir the contents, Kate stretched to see what he was cooking.

A tomato sauce, she speculated before hunching over the puzzle. Narrowing her eyes, she studied one puzzle piece. Shaped like antelope horns, it slid easily into an empty spot in the middle of the puzzle. "What is this a puzzle of?" She stared harder at the partially formed picture. Bright red and orange and yellow hot-air balloons. "A balloon race," she said more to herself than him. Most of the remaining pieces were blue. The sky, of course. Endless sky, she thought. He probably thrived on the challenge. "Why did you choose this particular puzzle?"

"It was the only one that the store had."

She picked up another piece, but glanced at him. "Not too particular, are you?"

"Very."

She glanced back again and caught his gaze directed at her backside. Straightening, she asked, "What's in the pot?"

"Spaghetti."

"And you cooked it?"

"Afraid?"

"Of your cooking?"

He laughed easily. "A smart man knows when to keep quiet."

"And you're a smart man."

"I invited you to dinner, didn't I?"

She sent him a quick grin. "Can I help?"

"Get the salad from the refrigerator."

She opened the refrigerator door, but looked back at the puzzle. "You'll never finish this," she said with a disgusted fling of her hand at all the blue pieces.

"I'll finish it. I never start anything that I don't finish."

She heard a promise in his voice, felt excitement skitter across her flesh in a warm shiver. She was tired of fighting what seemed inevitable. They'd make love. For one night, she wouldn't think too much. She'd enjoy whatever came her way. Falling in love was another matter. "Plates?"

He gestured toward the cabinet.

"Are you always successful in everything you start?"

"No one is." He drained the spaghetti and poured it into a bowl. "My marriage wasn't exactly a success story." He stilled and stared at the tangled pasta.

Kate inclined her head, hoping he'd say more about his marriage, but he crossed the room and yanked open the silverware drawer.

"I need a favor from you."

She stared expectantly at him.

"The banquet that I mentioned to you before is in need of a combo." At her nod, he went on, "You must know plenty of musicians."

"A few," she admitted, smiling as he closed the distance between them.

"Do I have to persuade you to help?"

Kate closed her eyes as he lowered his head. She didn't need to see. She felt his smiling lips playing across hers. She pressed closer, responding to the heat rising between them, to his tongue pushing the kiss to an intimate one that explored and savored. How had she lived without his taste before this? More importantly, she wondered if she could stand much more without knowing his touch. She trembled, wanting him to take her to a private world where only they would exist. A sweet pang of longing raced through her. She wanted his gentleness. And his hardness. They balanced each other perfectly, even in his kiss. She'd have forgotten dinner if he'd urged her to, but he drew back.

Lightly his lips caressed the curve of her jaw. "Give it some thought."

She felt weak and suddenly too vulnerable. "When you invited me here tonight, were you expecting . . . ?"

He touched her lips, silencing her, then turned away, leaving her standing alone and feeling limp.

"The sauce is ready," he announced.

Kate looked down at the bowl of pasta, which he'd set in her hands. Smooth. Too smooth, she mused. First entice, then pull away. Kate whirled around and carried the dish to the candlelit table in the adjacent room. He wouldn't do it again, she vowed. But who was she fooling? He could walk up to her right now, and she wouldn't resist. She wished she was better at playing games. If she were, she could hide what he made her feel. Instead, she walked around like some idiot carrying a billboard that announced every emotion he aroused.

Kate stilled and stared at one of the dining room paintings. Waves crashed against rocks beneath an ominous dark blue sky. A lone sailboat battled nature's adversity. She saw herself on that sailboat, heading toward the dock before the storm hit. She'd experienced many moments like that. Alone, she'd struggled against everyday conditions, wanting to get where she belonged. But she'd never known where that was. He'd always known. He'd always had people who cared about him. Yet he always seemed to understand what she was feeling. "Kate."

She turned.

He set the bowl of sauce on the table. "I didn't expect anything tonight. I wanted to be with you," he said softly. "Just be with you."

Men were liars, Brian thought later as he strolled into the kitchen with the dirty dishes. Of course, he'd been expecting something. And she knew it. He wanted her more than any other woman he knew, even more than he'd once wanted Diane. He'd been younger then, and explosive. But the wanting he felt for Kate was more powerful than anything he'd felt in his youth. He could have had her earlier if he'd pushed the moment. But he'd done enough pushing into her life. He needed her to want him, too.

He stood in the doorway and watched her circling his living room, and he couldn't think about anything but how soft she looked, how soft she'd felt. As she swung a glance back at him, he stood rooted to the spot, reminding himself that he'd lied. Now he was stuck with it. They couldn't sit down on the sofa. Hell, he didn't even dare stand close to her. "Do you play Ping-Pong?"

"Did you plan on challenging me to a game?"

A tangible barrier was what he needed, he decided as he recalled the silk teddy he'd touched earlier. "Don't try to hustle me, Kate. You're good, aren't you?"

She returned an impish smile. "I have to warn you, I do play a mean game."

Humor seemed a good safeguard. "Then the game will take longer," he said in challenge.

She laughed. "Before you lose?"

"Before you do."

Brian led the way into the basement, flicking on lights. "You might like to go to the banquet."

"I might," she returned airily while she strolled into the dark part of the basement.

He flicked on another light, illuminating the Ping-Pong table, and then handed her a paddle. "I have it on good authority that they're serving lime sherbet."

"Tempting." She looked around the room and saw mementos of youth everywhere: a faded pom-pom, a dozen baseballs with faded ink markings stating the dates of home runs, a collection of dolls, a small train waiting on a track that traversed a man-made mountain. On the sofa were delicately stitched needlepoint pillows. Equally as faded was a decades-old college pennant from Notre Dame.

"My father's," he said without being asked. "Are you ready?"

Kate moved to the opposite end of the table. "Don't plan to win this time."

"I'll win."

Kate noted his grin before he tapped the ball to her. They weren't discussing the same thing, she realized, and nearly missed the ball. She concentrated, guessing at the type of game he'd play. Though he returned the ball without any force, she sensed that he would play hard.

"Do you always have such thrilling jobs as climbing into garbage cans?" she asked, wondering if conversation distracted him, hoping it would.

"Sometimes I get to trail beautiful women."

She nearly missed the ball that he slammed at her. He quickened the pace suddenly and forced her to dive to the side to return a volley.

Thoughts of conversation were discarded, but Kate was aware of a different kind of advantage. She noted his gaze on her instead of the Ping-Pong ball. She took advantage of the opportunity and whacked the ball hard at him.

He missed the volley.

"My point." She blew out a breath. "Any excuse for missing that one?"

"Opponent distraction," he quipped in response to her smug grin.

"What did I do?"

"You moved."

She smiled first, then clucked her tongue. "A likely excuse."

As his eyes met hers, Kate served. The ball tipped the top of the net, forcing him to lunge and stretch to tip the ball back to her. He tapped it too hard.

Kate stood back and watched. The ball hit the floor, bounced four times and rolled to a stop at the other end of the basement.

"You cheat."

She laughed. It was so easy for him to make her laugh. It would be so easy for him to make her love. But look how falling in love had complicated her mother's life. It was an overrated emotion, Kate reminded herself.

Snowflakes were fluttering in the air during the drive from his house.

Brian glanced away from the street. "Don't gloat," he said in response to her smug grin.

She giggled. "You get very red in the face when you're losing. Did you know that?" she teased.

He braked in front of the Shamrock and then flicked off the ignition. "Did you ever hear of a gracious winner?"

As he narrowed his eyes at her, she giggled again. "Nope."

"Never again," he mumbled before getting out of the car, but he felt warmed inside by her youthful, exuberant mood. "Silliness becomes you," he murmured close to her ear when she stood on the sidewalk beside him.

"Does it?"

He bent his head and kissed her lightly on the mouth.

"What was that for?"

With an arm on her back, he turned her toward the restaurant. "A kiss for the winner."

"Thank you."

"Not you." He opened the door for her and brushed his lips across her temple. "Me."

Smoky, crowded and noisy, the dimly lit restaurant smelled of alcohol and tobacco. As Brian led the way around tables, Kate heard conversations highlighted by brogues and robust spurts of laughter. Lingering in the background were the sounds of a harmonica and a piano.

His fingers tight around her hand, Brian assured her, "You'll like it here. They serve green beer on St. Patrick's Day."

Greetings followed them, and she sensed the congeniality and camaraderie and warmth of regular customers—families and longtime friends.

The sweet smell of pipe tobacco drifted toward her. At a nearby table, a whiskered man puffed heartily on a curved stem.

"This way," Brian urged.

Kate glanced back at the man with the pipe.

"Is something wrong?"

"No." She sniffed again. "I like the smell of a pipe. When I was in the children's home, someone—I think he was with the state services—he smoked a pipe. A different tobacco, though, than this one."

"You like pipe smokers, huh?" He grimaced as if considering the idea.

Kate grinned up at him. "Not that much."

"Thank you for that one."

He led her to a table in a far corner. "Kate, this is Tom Malone."

Kate nodded at the introduction, barely able to hear their voices over someone's one-handed piano rendition of a Burt Bacharach tune.

Tom pulled out a chair for her. "It takes time to get used to Brian," he said in a stage whisper. "I'm still trying to after five years."

Brian grinned good-naturedly and took a chair next to hers. "As one of the men in blue, he has a grudging respect for private investigators."

"Your sister's here," Tom informed Brian while offering Kate a stranger's hesitant smile. "Beating the pants off of Uncle Charley in a dart game." He pushed back his chair. "And you'll never get a waitress tonight. It's too crowded. I'll sneak behind the bar and get you something."

"He's a policeman?" Kate asked when they were alone.

"Detective. Three-quarters of the people here work at the department. Tom's uncle owns this place. Charley worked at the department with my dad. Everybody sort of knows everybody here."

"I didn't realize help was so near. If I ever need it—"

He touched her hand. "Call me."

How easily she'd begun to rely on him, Kate realized. She sensed a danger to her heart, but couldn't seem to find a protective shield against the emotion he stirred within her.

"Here you are," Tom announced, cutting into her thoughts and setting two beers on the table. "Brian said that you're a music teacher."

Kate cast a questioning look at Brian.

"I forgot to tell you that Tom is psychic."

"What else did he tell you about me?" she asked, gesturing with her head toward Brian.

"That he nearly ruined your audition with some highbrow."

Kate supplied a name. "Boris Breshkov." She smiled at Brian. "He called and made an appointment with me for later this month," she announced, unable to veil her excitement.

"To audition again?"

"Yes, I was—" Kate hesitated as a feminine voice cut into their conversation.

"There you are." A tall, dark-haired woman said from a few feet away.

Brian game her an indulgent look. "I thought you were playing darts."

"I won." She smiled at Kate. "Hi, Kate," she said without waiting for an introduction.

Kate arched an eyebrow at Brian. "Someone else that you told about me?"

"She's a fortune-teller. My sister, Sabrina," he said as an introduction. "Kate doesn't look like Aunt Ethel, does she?"

Sabrina rested a hand on the back of Brian's chair. "A lovely but eccentric woman."

"All piano teachers are," Brian remarked, smiling teasingly at Kate.

"She really is," Sabrina went on. "She used to have a fat cat named Tabby. And her house always smelled. One of her students told her one day that her house smelled like elephants."

Tom laughed.

Sabrina shifted, offering him her back and facing Kate more squarely. A subtle but meaningful move, Kate thought.

Her head cocked, Sabrina said, "I meant to ask you, Brian. What happened to the blind in the office?"

"It died."

His sister sighed heavily. "You have the patience of a roadrunner. Kate, I heard that my impatient brother nearly ruined your audition with Breshkov."

"He told you, too?"

Brian looked away.

"He barrels through life," Sabrina quipped.

Kate already knew that.

Brian shoved back his chair and grabbed her hand. "Next, one of them will be telling you about the time that I poured soap down the street during a rainstorm."

Kate giggled. "You didn't?"

He pulled her to her feet. "Dance with me."

"Did you?" she persisted, following him past couples at the edge of a small dance floor.

"Tom told me that sometimes it's best to plead the Fifth. I was very young," he added.

"When I was young, I always shook Christmas presents."

"Did you?" He grinned. "I unwrapped them."

"That's criminal."

He laughed and gathered her in his arms as if she belonged there. "You say some of the most unexpected things."

"Am I amusing you?"

He kissed her palm. "Fascinating."

"Don't try charm now."

"Useless, huh?" he asked while he stroked her back in a caress that was as much a seduction as his kisses had been.

Tiny electrifying sparks shot down her spine. "It won't work."

"Even if I told you that you weaken my knees."

"Really?"

"Really."

As he tugged her closer, Kate curled a hand around the back of his neck and pressed her cheek against his. Why couldn't he be a pleasant memory in her life? She expected nothing more. She never expected too much. Few things in life were lasting. In the past she'd learned to take happiness as she'd found it. Why not now? Why not with him?

At the brush of his thigh, a warmth rushed through her. Earlier he'd told her that he expected nothing tonight. She should have been grateful that he wasn't pressuring her. Instead, she realized that she wanted to anticipate later. She wanted to let her emotions run free.

Chapter Eight

I've never liked this part of dating." Kate unlocked the door to her apartment. "It's such an uncomfortable time."

Brian's breath fanned the sensitive skin below her ear. "Is the man usually breathing down your neck?"

Kate laughed and swung a look back at him. "Yes."

"And eager to be asked in." He stroked her cheek with his knuckles. "Don't blame him for trying with you, Kate. He sees softness. He sees hair that makes him think of silk. He smells a scent that will linger with him forever."

She took a deep breath and turned to face him. "You're always doing that."

"Doing what?"

Her nerves jumped as he caressed the outline of her lips with a fingertip. "Saying things."

"Real bad things, huh?"

Nothing felt steady. Not her breathing or her pulse or her legs.

"You're tempting."

"In what way?"

"You make me want to kiss you until your legs weaken."

"That's the first-date syndrome," she mused.

"First date? This isn't our first date." He gathered her to him and rested his hands on her back. "On a first date, most men don't feel as if they're going to go mad from wanting."

She stepped closer and ran her fingers along the short stubble of his beard. Bristles pricked her flesh. "You don't think this is a typical first date?"

"Hardly. We've already shared a pizza."

He'd spoken lightly, casually, but she watched his eyes turn dark with desire's tenseness. "No, you ate it, and I watched." Her hands crept around his neck. "In amazement," she added.

"We went grocery shopping," he reminded her while pushing open the door behind her. "Chose grapes together." He urged her to take a step back into the apartment. "Folded laundry."

She giggled in the darkness of the room.

His lips brushed the curve of her jaw. "Took a trip."

"I remember." Kate tilted her head back to give his mouth freedom to explore her throat. *You held me while I cried,* she reflected.

Slowly he unbuttoned her coat. "I told you that I expected nothing tonight," he said between gentle nips at her lips.

"But if I asked you..." she managed while unzipping his jacket to reach the buttons of his shirt. "If I asked, you'd want to stay, wouldn't you?"

He released a muffled laugh against her throat.

Kate tugged his shirttail from his pants. "Maybe you should shut the door." She heard the click before she completed the sentence.

Her arms tightened around his neck as she pushed aside niggling concerns that had bothered her for too long about where emotions for him would lead her. All that mattered was the moment. Desire swept wildly through her. Her fingers crept up across his stomach muscles to his broad chest. He felt wonderful. Strong and masculine. Sleek. Warm. "I know that you're not expecting anything..."

He looked down at his opened shirt and let out a long breath. "I'd stay."

"If I asked?"

She nearly moaned with the need building within her as he slid down the zipper of her jumpsuit and his cold knuckles brushed her flesh.

"How much time will it take to make a decision?" he asked in a voice hoarser sounding than usual.

"All night," she murmured, yanking at the buckle of his belt. The jumpsuit slid from her shoulders to her ankles in a slow, slithering motion. She felt the coolness of the room on her bare back, on her breasts as he pushed the wispy silk away from them. Her breath caught in her throat when he tucked his thumbs into the top of her panties. Kate shook her head, then gasped at the touch of his fingers sliding downward. The silk panties followed with a whisper.

She closed her eyes, letting her senses take over. She heard the rustle of denim, she felt the moist caress of his tongue on her shoulder, she tasted the sweetness of him when his tongue plunged into her mouth. Her body swayed toward him. The hard contours of his bare flesh suddenly pressed against her. She wanted to touch; she needed to. Beneath her hands she felt the muscles and planes of his back, the tautness of his buttocks, the heat that flamed from within.

As if she had no will of her own, she followed the command of his hands, her arms coiling tighter around his neck when he slid an arm beneath her knees. A chill raced over her flesh as they journeyed through the cool darkness of the rooms.

"I've ached for you," he murmured against her shoulder, lowering her to the bed.

Her face inches from his, she searched his eyes. Passion filled them. They looked fierce. Yet he had such softness about him. He gave so much, so easily. She'd never been given so much emotion so freely. Even now, he hadn't insisted on anything in return. She'd needed him. If she hadn't made the first move, she sensed he'd have left without pressuring her. And by doing so, he'd seduced her.

His hands framed her face. The kiss warmed her with its gentleness, filling her with pleasure. Her tongue met his and explored. She expected him to rush her. She felt his need against her thigh, but he showed a patience she'd seen at no other time in him. He wasn't a patient man. She knew that. She'd seen him push and prod and barrel forward into her life. And yet, he offered now the sensuous slowness of a lover who cherished and treasured what he'd insisted on finding.

Her breathing grew ragged as she touched him. Discovering everything seemed such a part of the moment. Her body molded to the strong, callused hands gliding slowly across her breasts, down her belly, between her thighs. Her blood pounded as he caressed, tormented, pleasured.

Masterful hands took her to the edge of desperation while his mouth nibbled her breasts. He spoke softly, murmuring her name, uttering unintelligible words. She didn't need to hear them, understand them, to know their meaning. Her body swelled with a wanting that left her breathless.

Gentleness gave way to a fury of need. She couldn't get enough of him, though his hands never stilled and his tongue never retreated from its intent to drive her to a writhing madness. Relentless in his play across her flesh, he stretched her control to its limit.

A melody began in her mind, its beat thudding harder with each kiss he placed on her flesh, with each moist flick of his tongue gliding across her body in the manner that fingertips slid down a keyboard. She arched to meet the gentle demand of a masterful conductor. Sounds, soft and urgent, slipped from her lips as she practiced music of her own on his flesh.

But the time wasn't meant for a solo. Breaths, moans, caresses mingled in a duet. When his lips returned to hers again, she opened her mouth, drawing in his tongue, feeling drugged by his taste, commanded by the rapid beat of his heart, enticed by the harshness of his breath. She blended with him when he lowered himself to her, tugging her hips closer. Her arms and legs embraced him, and an orchestration as old as time began. They moved against each other, the slowness, the tenderness slipping away. His mouth ground into hers with an urgent, hard message. Restless, she answered his relentlessness, her body moving against and with his, drawing him deeper, filling herself with him until they shuddered with the fierceness of the passionate beat.

Kate listened to sounds, her own breathing as harsh and unsteady as his. They'd come together like beautiful music. They'd each played and stroked the other as if given the gift of a perfectly tuned instrument. The piece had built to a passionate crescendo. But Kate was suddenly aware that she'd heard a softer melody, too, the lingering one of a love song.

Brian lay in a jumble of sheets, the weight of Kate's head on his shoulder. He considered moving. Only considered it. The brush of her fingers across his chest held him still. He shifted to curl an arm beneath her and draw her closer. She'd been so giving. When she'd shuddered with him, her soft moans filling his mind, he'd felt the wonder, the excitement, the weakness and the power that he'd known his first time.

Despite the mantle of darkness surrounding them, he could see her face. She snuggled closer, accepting the tightness of his arms around her. Yet he forced himself to ask. "Want me to leave?"

"Why?" she asked so softly that he barely heard her.

"You have neighbors," he murmured, closing his eyes as the notion of sleep tempted him.

"Everyone has neighbors."

"I'll stay then."

"Yes, stay." She melted against him.

"Until later?" he said softly, as heat began to flow through his body when she pressed her mouth against his chest. In lazy circles her tongue joined the play. Excitement spiraled through him. Not for the first time, he reflected. With a kiss, she'd excited him. For forever it seemed he had wanted to make love to her. But the longing had blossomed. Then, he had yearned as a man desires the feminine body, but the joining of flesh had merely symbolized what had existed within him for her. He understood desire's spontaneity. He knew how to control its stunning edge. It warned and prepared a man with its taut pulsing and building need. But the heart was more merciless. Delicate, sensitive, it waited. It opened. It welcomed, unprotected.

He caressed her hair. He watched her eyes close, her mouth inching lower down his chest, and even as the distracting storm began to build within him, he longed to say words, simple words. Difficult words.

They remained unsaid. But he wondered at what moment she had become more important to him than anything or anyone else.

He touched the sharp point of her hip, the softness of her thighs, the warmth between them. He felt a weakness flood him. A desperation returned to bury himself in her as her legs parted, to feel the heat rise in her body again.

But she shifted, snatched air from him with a simple touch. Inching down, she froze him. Her fingertips grazed him with a slow, tantalizing stroke.

"Much later," she whispered, pushing up and away from him.

He stopped breathing, his gaze dropping to the delicate fingers caressing and fluttering across him. He felt possessed. She seared his flesh, branding her claim on him. He knew he was lost. He knew that he'd never be able to take a step away from her now. His body quivered in anticipation as she sat up on her knees. Moonlight played over her bare skin, casting a silver light across the paleness of her shoulder. He felt strands of her hair brush the tops of his thighs, then he closed his eyes as he was swept up in a fierce wave of sensations, in breathless moments that spiraled him toward the brink of sanity.

He waited until the choice wasn't his any longer. His pulse racing, he rolled her beneath him and took her with him on a journey filled with madness, with trembling pleasure, with the love he felt for her.

Noise. An indistinguishable sound awakened him. Brian stared at the bright, sunlit ceiling and frowned. "What is that?" he questioned out loud to himself.

"Awful, isn't it?"

He turned his head on the pillow.

Her chin propped on her hand, Kate smiled at him. "I thought you were dead."

He raised his head to kiss her. "Good morning."

Soundly, she moved her lips across his in a slow, enticing manner, her tongue briefly touching the tip of his.

Brian dropped his head back onto the pillow. "What a way to start the day."

A pleasurable expression settled on her face. "I did think you were dead. I couldn't imagine anyone sleeping through that noise."

Brian frowned again. "What is that?"

"But you snore," she said instead of answering him.

"I don't snore."

"Yes, you do."

"Forget my snoring. It can't be as bad as—" The noise stopped.

She tilted her head, responding to the sudden silence.

"It sounded like a cat," Brian said speculatively.

She shook her head.

"It did."

"No, it didn't."

"Someone's cat—"

"No pets allowed."

"Then, I—" Brian stopped and listened as the noise began again. "I can't stand this," he said, swinging his legs out of the bed.

As he stood, he looked back at her. "Aren't you getting up?"

She grinned, her eyes sweeping down his body. "No."

"How can you do that?"

"I'm not the snoop. You are." She huddled deeper under the covers. "I'm going back to sleep."

He pointed a finger at her. "Don't move. I'll be back." Briefly, he glanced at the bathrobe hanging on a hook in her closet. He'd look lousy in a yellow robe, especially one with lace. He decided to take his chances that the odd noise wouldn't result in his having to exit her apartment in his birthday suit.

Kate wished she had a camera. She smiled at the sight of him standing by the apartment door, peeking out of it. One good nudge and he'd be in the hallway, resplendently naked. "Well, Mike Hammer, what's going on?"

Brian waved back at her to be quiet.

"Who's making the noise?" she whispered, playing along with his spy game.

He looked over his shoulder at her and frowned. "What's this?" he asked, plucking at the lapel of her robe. "You weren't supposed to get dressed."

"I didn't." Enticingly, Kate fanned back a flap of her robe to reveal a bare leg.

Nodding as if satisfied that she hadn't upset his plans, he again peered out the door.

Kate stood on her toes and peeked over his shoulder.

"Your friend is nuts," he whispered.

Kate slapped a hand over her mouth to stifle a giggle. "Oh, Harry," she said low on a laugh.

Standing outside Liz's apartment door, Harry strummed away on a banjo and sang out an off-key rendition of "Let Me Call You Sweetheart."

"What the hell does he think he's doing?" Brian asked.

"Serenading her?"

"He'll be lucky if she doesn't throw a bucket of water at him."

"It's cute." Kate stepped back and perused Brian's backside. "So are you." Lightly she traced a fingertip down the back of his thigh.

He jumped and swung a deadly serious look at her despite her actions. "Are you sure that your neighbor isn't married to a loony?"

"Always the detective." She rolled her eyes. "I'm sure."

He closed the door quietly, then turned to face her. "Then I'll mind my own business." He grinned and tugged at the tie on her robe.

"What are you doing?" Kate asked laughingly.

"Do you need an explanation?"

She giggled again. "You always make me do that," she said, trying to stifle a grin.

"Do what?"

"Laugh." Kate watched his brow knit.

"Laughter is good for you," he told her, but his frown deepened.

Kate looked down at the tight little knot that had formed from his yanking on the tie. She watched in amusement as he tugged even harder. "I never properly thanked you for the teapot." She roamed kisses across his face.

"I think you did," he returned on a grin, but he didn't look up.

"You're tightening it." Even as she made the comment, she felt the belt of the robe loosen.

His hands slid inside her robe and intimately ran over her hips to her bottom. "I'm hungry. Incredibly hungry."

"Self-indulgence is supposed to be decadent."

"So we'll be decadent," he whispered, warming her breast with his breath.

"Yes." Kate caressed his head. "Yes."

"These should be ready in a jiffy," Brian said while whisking the eggs later that morning.

Kate stopped by the table and stared at her morning newspaper strewn across it. She shuffled sections. "Where are the headlines?"

Brian glanced back. "I don't know."

"Didn't you read it?" She eyed the coffee streaming into the glass pot. It looked five times stronger than what she usually made.

"I read the basketball scores."

"You went all the way down three flights of stairs for the newspaper so you could read the basketball scores?"

"I read what's important to me."

"What else? *Spider-man?*"

"The best way to start the day."

"Your poor brain." As he turned to look at her over his shoulder, she feigned a sympathetic look. "Atrophy."

He grinned. "What do you read first? The stock quotations?"

Kate riffled through the newpaper until she found the front section. "A brief glance at the headlines wouldn't hurt."

"I know the Nuggets won again."

"Not the sports headlines," she countered. "Two convicts broke out of prison this morning. Did you know that?"

"Where? Colorado?"

Kate glanced back down at the paper to skim the article. She made a face. "Utah."

Humor danced in his eyes.

Kate settled her hips on the table and watched him pour a small amount of milk into the bowl. "You really do like to cook, don't you?"

"Yeah."

"You'd make a good wife."

He chuckled. "Or a great husband?"

"Are you an advocate for everyone being married?"

"Why not? It's good to share your life with someone else."

She ambled toward him and then leaned sideways, setting her forearm on the counter and tilting her head so she could see his face better. Beneath the morning sunlight streaming into the room, his hair was a dark, rich mahogany color. Lightly she touched a strand of it behind his ear. "I didn't think you'd feel that way."

"Why?"

"Because you don't talk about your marriage. You act as if the subject is off limits."

"Do you have questions?"

"I'm curious."

"Ask." He turned a steady gaze on her. "That's all *you* ever had to do."

"It wasn't an amicable divorce, was it?"

"Few are. I met Diane in college." He cast her an odd smile. "At a music recital. We both liked music, although she was trained like you are."

"What did she play?"

"A cello. Extremely well," he added. "After we were married, she was always involved in committees to help the symphony or aid struggling young musicians."

"Tell me about before," Kate said, sensing that she'd never understand him unless she knew something about the woman he'd once loved.

"We shared something in common. One date led to another. Everything seemed perfect. Then one weekend she invited me to meet her parents." He stopped whisking the eggs. "I wasn't prepared. I should have been. She drove a Porsche, wore Gucci shoes, lived in an expensive apartment away from campus. But nothing prepared me for the mausoleum that her parents called home. Or prepared me for her parents."

"They didn't like you right away?"

"They expected her to bring home some nice blue-blooded male who traveled in the same circle, not an Irish cop's son." He gave her a quick grin and resumed whisking. "Her mother was polite. Her father hated me. But I didn't want to marry him, so the feeling was mutual."

Kate smiled suddenly.

He saw it and frowned. "What just went through your mind?"

"That opposition probably made you even more determined."

"It did. For both of us. Despite that disastrous weekend, she was as eager as I was to keep seeing each other. I thought she wanted everything I did. We rushed into marriage after knowing each other only three months. I could blame that impulsiveness on youth, but what's the point. The marriage lasted a year."

Kate looked into the bowl at the yellow liquid. "Add a pinch of sugar."

"Why?"

"Just do it. Liz told me to make them that way." As he reached for the sugar bowl, she asked, "What caused the marriage to end?"

"She couldn't live without the money. And her father kept pushing it at us. Every time he did, I'd refuse it. She wanted it. It was a vicious circle."

Kate wasn't surprised. She'd guessed that he was a proud man.

"And we didn't have much money."

Reason made his statement seem odd. "You were in school."

"And married. I couldn't ask her to live on hot dogs and beans. She was used to caviar and champagne."

"Before marriage, she must have realized that her life would be different."

"I don't think either of us gave anything much thought. But I knew I couldn't stay in college. I left—" At Kate's frown, he added, "I never regretted leaving. I started working with my dad at the agency, but even working full-time, I couldn't compete with what her father offered her."

"You know what he sounds like."

"I know what he was." Brian offered a weak smile. "Unbelievably autocratic. And he never acknowledged that I existed. Over and over again, he gave her things I couldn't afford. He wasn't just being generous. He wanted his little girl back. Eventually, he won."

"She left?"

"That's the way it went."

"I'm not getting you on the rebound, am I?"

He whipped around. "Don't even think that." His look was puzzled. "Why would you even ask that question?"

"Morning-after jitters."

"Don't have them," he assured her, his voice softening. "No," he answered, "I won't say that I stopped loving her right away. I'd be lying. It took a while before everything became just a memory. Lately..." He dropped the whisk into the bowl and took a step toward her. "Lately it seems as if I was never in love with her or married. Possibly real love comes only once."

The tinny sound of Harry's banjo suddenly sounded again from the hallway. Kate used the distraction to avoid conflicting feelings too difficult to face. "I don't believe it," she said, noting the seriousness hadn't left Brian's gaze. "An encore." Suddenly uneasy, she turned away to drop bread into the slots of the toaster. "The man is crazy."

"Or love is in the air." His whisper fanned her ear as he lifted her hair to kiss the back of her neck.

With a few words, he'd set off a fuse of panic within her. She didn't want to hear the words she sensed might come next. She wasn't ready to hear them. She tensed.

"Hey?"

"Brian, don't push this," she appealed when he grasped her upper arms and turned her to face him. "Let us go along whatever way works."

He frowned.

"I don't give up the kind of control of my life that you're asking for."

"I'm not asking for control."

"I don't know that," she said, shrugging her shoulders to ease herself from his grip.

"I told you that I'm not."

Kate shook her head and backed away.

"Try trusting me."

"I might break something."

"That's not your exclusive risk, Kate."

His gaze clashed with hers for a long moment, but he took several steps back in a reassuring gesture.

Not quite steady, she jumped instinctively at the sound of the door buzzer. Kate shot a glance at the clock. "Oh, no."

"What now?"

"You've got to go." She rushed forward and shoved him toward the doorway.

He released a quick, short laugh. "What . . . ?"

"Get dressed." Kate placed her hands on his back to propel him forward. "You've got to go," she insisted. The stubbornness of his stance made her feel as if she were trying to shove a two-ton truck by herself.

Brian stopped in the doorway, refusing to budge. "Who's here?"

"Lisa." As he stared dumbly at her, she said in a slow, measured manner. "Estelle Manington's daughter?"

"Again?"

"Again."

He grimaced. "I left five minutes ago." He kissed her hard before rushing toward the bedroom for his shoes. "I'll call you later."

Brian tossed a wad of paper across the room. It dropped short of the wastebasket.

"Your aim is bad this morning," Sabrina quipped while closing one of her desk drawers.

"No, my timing is."

"Are you still seeing her?"

"Seeing who?"

"Don't play stupid. I guessed that you were seeing her regularly."

"How?"

"You've been whistling every morning."

"I'm a happy person."

She snorted, then asked more seriously, "Are you done with the case?"

"Not quite." He thumbed through a Rolodex to hunt for the Stranton phone number. He picked up the telephone receiver, then dropped it back on its cradle. "Damn, I wish I could forget the Strantons and their involvement with her."

"Why? Was your timing off this morning?"

"She's wary."

"Kate is? I'd be wary of you, too."

Brian grinned. "She's had an odd life, Brie, yet..." He shook his head. "Never mind." He picked up the receiver. He'd done it again. He'd fallen in love with a woman who could be wrong for him. How could he explain that to his sister, to anyone?

Brian announced himself and then shuffled papers while he waited for the sound of Gertrude Stranton's voice.

"Mr. Fleming?"

"Yes, Mrs. Stranton. I learned something yesterday that you might be interested in."

She responded with vague answers to his story about Madeline Lindstrom being employed at her husband and late brother-in-law's law firm.

"What is she like? Katherine?"

"Lovely." Brian released a deep sigh. "She'd dedicated. I told you that she teached music, mostly piano. She's sensitive, she—laughs easily. She loves silly things like green food and collects teapots and—" Brian stopped himself. What the hell was he doing? "She's a nice woman," he said in a businesslike tone. "And she's confused."

"Does she want to know the truth?"

"I don't think she believes that she does."

"But you think so?"

"I'd find it difficult not to believe someone would want to know their true identity."

"But you haven't proven that she is my..." Her voice trailed off as if she wasn't sure what relationship she might have with Kate. "A relative of mine?"

"It's possible that I'd never be able to prove that. All I can do, Mrs. Stranton, is present information to you."

A vague pounding in his head turned into a throbbing headache before he finished the call. Frowning, he rummaged through the top drawer of his desk for aspirin.

"Will you stop that?" Sabrina scolded. "How can I concentrate with you making all that noise?"

"Have you got any aspirin?"

"There's a bottle in the bathroom." As he shuffled into the adjacent room, she called out, "What exactly is wrong?"

"Plenty." Brian gulped down two pills. He leaned against the doorjamb. "Stranton was curious."

"So?"

"About Kate. About the kind of woman she is."

"She's probably beginning to accept the idea that Kate might be a relative. That's what that means."

Brian drained the water in the glass. "The closer I get to the Strantons' connections with Madeline Lindstrom, the more I want to stop this investigation."

"Brian, she has a right to know if she is..."

Brian raised a halting hand. "I know that. But I can tell that she's getting confused. And what will she feel if she does learn that she's a Stranton."

"Nobody knows how someone else will respond to such news."

"Or act after finding out."

Sabrina inclined her head questioningly.

"Diane and I might have made it if her family hadn't always been waving their money in her face."

"Brian—"

He sent her a quieting glare.

"Okay, okay. I'm sure whatever I say is going to fall on deaf ears."

A defensive edge entered his voice. "I'm not bullheaded, Brie."

Sabrina nodded. "Of course you're not."

* * *

Kate stood in her apartment doorway and watched Estelle and Lisa Manington waddle toward the staircase. At twelve, the young girl had already inherited her mother's pear shape, tilted chin and shrill voice. Kate made a half turn toward her apartment, but stilled at the sight of Liz peeking her head out of the door.

"Is the coast clear?" she said in a stage whisper.

Kate smiled and nodded, gesturing for Liz to join her.

On tiptoe, Liz ran down the hallway. "I feel like a thief."

Kate held the door for her. "Come in and tell me what Harry is doing."

"Romancing me," she said with incredulity. "Do you believe this?"

"You have a lot of history together."

"I don't know what he wants, Katie. Yesterday he sent me flowers. My apartment looks like a florists' convention."

Kate touched her shoulder. "Terrible."

"It is." Her eyes widened. "And *you*? What have you been up to?"

"Up to?"

"Oh, so innocent. If you aren't careful, you could end up like this," she said, pointing a finger to her chest. "I'm married to a man who is nuts with a capital *N*."

Kate flopped back on an overstuffed chair. Listening to Liz exaggerate always lightened her mood.

"So your private investigator is still around. And everything is okay?" At Kate's silence, she rambled on, "He was here all— Sorry, I'm not supposed to notice overnight guests."

Kate's smile waned. "It's not what you think."

"Of course not." Liz pulled a face and shook her head. "He just pumps your blood."

"Yes, he does do that," Kate admitted on a laugh.

"He's so great-looking that he makes your legs weak."

"That, too."

"So you're hung up on him? What's wrong with that? I know what you said yesterday. But I don't understand your reluctance. Admit you're in love. Enjoy."

Kate stacked magazines on the end table beside her, avoiding Liz's perceptive eyes.

"He has a dangerous job, doesn't he?"

"I don't think so," Kate answered. "From what he's told me, which hasn't been a lot about his work, he spends more time sitting in cars and watching unfaithful spouses than doing something as thrilling as finding a Maltese Falcon."

"Okay, let's do this systematically." At Kate's questioning look, Liz added, "Every couple has a problem."

"We don't have one."

Liz squinted at her. "Then . . . ?"

Too easy, Kate wanted to say. Love had come too easy. At least for her.

Liz snapped her fingers in front of Kate's eyes. "He's obviously made a move on you."

"You're adorable, but totally tactless."

"A little more respect, please. I am a few years older than you."

"Yes, Granny."

"Not that much, thank you."

"Are you going back to Harry?" Kate rose to her feet.

Liz looked pained. "I don't know, Katie. I wasn't too thrilled with being left in the first place. Now I'm just supposed to forgive and forget?"

"I don't know the answer."

"Who does? But you—" Liz placed her hands on Kate's shoulders "—you are in the wonderful throes of passion."

Kate started to deny it, then gave in to the joy warming her. "Yes, I am."

Liz's hands came together in a clap. "How wonderful. Katie's in love."

Kate managed a smile, but the idea scared her. All her life she'd wanted love. And now that she might finally have found it, she felt like running.

Brian strolled through the quiet lobby that led to the offices of Wendell and Stranton and Associates. Every corner he turned announced old, established wealth. He kept walking until he reached the back of the building and a small office.

An old man looked up from the stack of mail he was sorting. "Have you got permission to be walking around here?"

Brian stepped forward and flashed his license at him.

"A private investigator?" He squinted at Brian's wallet. "Like Columbo?"

"He was a police lieutenant."

The old man scratched his head.

"I'd like to ask a few questions for an investigation I'm handling," Brian said louder to be heard over the whistling of a teakettle.

"You want to ask *me* questions?"

"I think you could be helpful."

The old man's face crinkled with his smile. "Guess that it would be all right. I'm on a break right now anyhow. This is my time." He swiveled his chair away from one desk to face another.

"Have you worked here long?"

"Forty-nine years." He dunked a tea bag into a cup of steaming water. "I'll be retiring soon. In two weeks." He continued dunking the tea bag. "I started working here when I was sixteen."

"You've probably seen a lot."

"Sure have."

"And you probably know every person who ever worked here."

"I delivered the mail to every desk until three years ago. Now I sort, and Micky delivers." He gestured toward a gawky-looking youth who'd tugged at his tie ten times in the past two minutes. "Mr. Stranton did that for me."

"Douglas Stranton?"

"He let me work a couple more years and train Micky. Mr. Stranton is a fine man. I haven't been too well, but he insisted I be allowed to stay so I could retire with a good pension."

Brian grimaced as the old man added a third packet of sugar to his tea. "Do you remember a woman named Madeline Lindstrom. She worked here about . . ."

"I don't need her life history, boy. I remember Maddie."

"You do?"

"I ain't senile, just old." The man's eyes lit up. "She was a real fine-looking woman."

Brian smiled and settled his hips back on a counter. "What do you remember about her?"

Kate watched Billy Newman's pudgy fingers pause on the keyboard. A tiny frown creased his eight-year-old forehead as he repeated the measure.

"You have to practice more between lessons," Kate scolded softly. "Listen to the metronome. One, two, three, four."

He mouthed the notes. C-C, E-E, G-G, C . . .

"That's right," Kate assured him. "Practice more at home, though." As Kate stopped the metronome, he jumped from the piano bench.

"Did you make cookies?"

Kate tousled his hair. "Yes. Let's go in the kitchen."

Fifteen minutes later, full of cookies, he grinned broadly, revealing the gap where a front tooth was missing. "I'll practice more. I promise."

"Good." Kate started to walk with him toward the door, but the ringing of the phone halted her in midstride. "Be careful going home," she called out before reaching for the receiver. Responding to his wave, she smiled as she spoke. "Hello."

"Katherine Lindstrom?"

"Yes."

A brief silence rattled Kate.

"Who is this?" she demanded.

The answer to her question swayed her. Kate reached back for the chair, then eased herself down into it, feeling as if her world were spinning.

Chapter Nine

One step into Kate's apartment and Brian knew something was wrong. She looked pale, stunned; her movements were mechanical as she turned toward a chair.

He heard the strain in her voice. "I had a phone call."

Brian took a step closer.

"From Gertrude Stranton."

He held his breath, not sure if his concern was for her or for himself.

"She wants to see me."

He took another step toward her, hesitated, then enveloped her protectively in his arms.

"I'm scared."

Me, too, he realized.

"They never bothered with me before. They didn't care."

Brian shoved aside his own emotions. "That's what you'll find out, whether or not they really do care."

"Why? Why now?"

"I don't think Gertrude Stranton ever knew that a child might exist somewhere."

"If Dorothy Arneson hadn't written to her..." Kate leaned back to look up at him.

"Yes, she started it." He hesitated again, and then continued. "I went to the law firm today, Kate."

Her eyes clouded with questions.

"Your mother was seeing one of the men there."

"Be specific," she insisted.

"A bigwig."

"A Stranton?"

"Yes."

"Douglas Stranton?"

"I don't know if it was Gertrude Stranton's husband or not, Kate."

"But does she? Is that why she called? Did he finally admit to her that he'd paid for a child he hadn't wanted?"

Brian held her firmly, sensing if he didn't that she'd pull away from him. Wasn't this what had bothered him from the moment that he'd learned she might be related to the Strantons?

"Did you call her and tell her what you learned?"

"No." He shook his head. "I haven't called her yet to give her that information."

Kate looked skeptical. "What if Gertrude Stranton is asking me to her home to tell me that she doesn't believe anything you've uncovered?" She drew a sharp breath. "I don't know what to think. I can't deal with this, Brian."

"Kate, Listen to me."

"I don't want to." She looked up, her eyes filled with the same appeal he'd heard in her voice.

"I'll go with you."

She insisted on distance, putting her hands against his chest and shoving herself away from him. "I'm not even sure that I'm going."

He was unable to help her, he realized as he watched her stroll to the window.

"I've lived this long without a family, without any of them." She wrapped her arms around herself. "I lived so many years feeling as if no one wanted me."

Brian bridged the space between them and whirled her around to face him.

Her mouth twisted in a self-deprecating smile. "No matter what she says, I have my own life. What's the point in seeing her?"

He raised his hands to her face. With his thumbs he smoothed hair away from her cheeks. She looked younger and more vulnerable at that moment than he'd ever seen her. "You want to," he said softly.

"No."

The youthful uncertainty in her voice constricted his throat. For endless seconds she stood perfectly still in his arms, then he felt her tear. Only one. But her raw pain was his. "Kate, cry. Let it out."

"No. No tears. I cried more than enough as a child. No more now," she said, brushing her lips across his cheek.

He plunged a hand into her hair, letting the strands twist around his fingers. He knew the softness beneath her strength, the seductiveness beneath her sweetness. He closed his eyes and buried his face in her hair. And he ached for her.

* * *

Snow glistened beneath the morning sunlight as Kate gazed out the bedroom window at the fresh carpet covering the ground. "It's beautiful outside." Behind her she heard the rasp of Brian's zipper, the snap of his jeans, the squeak of floorboards as he approached.

Splaying a palm over her belly, he pulled her back. "It's beautiful inside."

Kate laid her head back on his shoulder. Featherlight, his tongue traced a slow path along her earlobe and around the shell of her ear. She turned her face into her shoulder. "That tickles."

"It's supposed to."

"Behave. Enjoy the view."

"I am," he murmured, and kissed the curve of her neck. "You enjoy the view and then later you can help me shovel a sidewalk."

"Don't think about the bad part of it."

"It's my nature. Too much black Irish in me."

"What does black Irish in a person make him do?"

"Oh, say dumb things like 'don't plant the potatoes—they might not grow.'"

Kate giggled and pretended to swat at her ear to stop his lips as they continued to play across it.

"I have to leave." He sighed and reluctantly pulled away.

Kate lounged against the window frame to watch him finish dressing.

Looking down as he buttoned his shirt, he asked, "Have you decided, Kate?"

"No."

He tucked the shirt into his jeans. "I'll meet you there."

Kate folded her arms across her chest. "I'm not going to delude myself," she said to his back when he reached for his jacket.

He looked back, studying her. "You'll never know what you have to make a choice about unless you go."

Kate remained silent. How could she explain she was afraid? Afraid of rejection. "I told you—"

"If you go," he said, interrupting her, "I'll be outside waiting for you." He took two steps away, then looked back again. "Okay?"

"Okay," she agreed softly. "If I go."

Kate fought her own thoughts, dealing with frustration and annoyance in her usual way. She scrubbed the bathroom floor; she riffled through the refrigerator, dumping moldy cheese and a two-week-old hamburger patty into the garbage; she scrubbed grease from the inside of her oven.

The usual method refused to work.

Then she took a long bath, thumbed through several magazines and pounded out "Heart and Soul" on the piano.

Again, nothing. She still felt tense, annoyed and afraid.

"Take a walk," she ordered herself, and grabbed her coat from the hall closet, wishing she had at least one lesson to give that day. But it was Wednesday. Wednesdays were her days. She usually loved them. But then nothing about today was usual.

She flicked off the television set on the way to the door. "I'll go grocery shopping and buy pistachio nuts," she mumbled while double-checking the locked door. "Do something."

"Not a good sign, Katie."

Kate jumped and whirled around.

Liz grinned. "Talking to yourself is not good news."

"I thought it was acceptable as long as I didn't answer myself."

"That's what crazy people tell themselves."

Kate smiled. "Are you coming or going?"

"Going."

"I'll walk down the stairs with you. Where are you headed?"

Liz sighed. "A big party."

Kate noted that she looked tired. "You work too hard."

"Do I?"

Kate slid an arm around her. "Do you need a sympathetic shoulder?"

"Oh, Katie. No one can help. I have to make my own decision. But even when Harry isn't around, I'm haunted by thoughts of him and the love we shared."

Kate gave her shoulder a squeeze. "You'll make the right decision."

"I hope so."

So will I. Kate stepped outside with her. With a wave, they parted, going in opposite directions. Feeling young and indecisive, Kate pushed the toe of a boot into the blanket of fresh snow. If she didn't see Gertrude Stranton, she might never know the truth. And she'd never get past the bitterness that was buried inside her. It existed, she admitted honestly. How could it not? She'd been abandoned. No one had wanted her all those years. That was one fact that nothing anyone said to her would ever change.

* * *

"Did you get the musicians yet?" Tom asked.

Brian grimaced and shifted the telephone receiver to his other ear while he reached for the address of a new client. "Not yet. But I will."

"You've only got a little more time."

"I will," Brian flared.

Tom was silent.

Brian leaned back in his chair. "I will," he said in a calmer voice.

Although he concentrated on fielding Tom's questions about musicians, the banquet music seemed a trivial problem. If Kate became a part of the Strantons' lives, a gap would form between them and would grow wider with each day that passed. And, dammit, he wanted to stop it now. Right now. But for her sake, for everything she'd wanted in life and had never had, he couldn't do anything but wait. He was lousy at waiting.

Dressed and ready to leave, Kate sighed at the sight of snowflakes rushing toward the ground. She slid into her coat in a methodical manner, as if every movement were well thought out. She hoped that she remained as calm during the next few hours.

Aware of her troubled thoughts, she doubted that she'd be able to concentrate on driving and phoned a taxi. She felt her stomach flip-flop. An early darkness seemed to parallel her late-afternoon mood. She quelled a twinge of panic and then dialed Brian's office number.

"Fleming Investigations," a female voice responded.

Dumbly Kate stood still for a second. She'd expected Brian's voice, the gruff foggy sound that seemed to have such a soothing effect on her.

"Hello? Is anyone there?"

"Is this Sabrina?"

"Yes," she answered brightly. "Who...?"

"Is Brian there?"

A silent second passed. "Kate? Kate, Brian's not here. Do you want to leave a message for him? He's on surveillance work, but he'll probably be done before early evening."

"He said that he'd meet me somewhere."

"Uh-huh."

"Would you tell him that I decided to go?"

Kate could almost hear the wheels turning in the woman's mind. "Yes, I will."

"Tell him to meet me at the—" Kate listened to the scratching sound of a pencil. When it stopped, she added, "At the Strantons'."

Tension coiled around her like a tight spring. Kate stood in the elegant hallway and waited for Gertrude Stranton. At the maid's footsteps echoing through the high-ceilinged rooms, Kate clutched the straps of her purse and took a deep, long breath. She doubted that she'd remember much of the surroundings other than impressions of antiques, massive gilt-edged mirrors and the glittering chandeliers. They spilled light across the maid as she returned and beckoned Kate to follow her.

Tall double doors stood open and led into a drawing room of muted grays and blues and silk-upholstered sofas and chairs.

A woman rose from one of them. Her face composed, her silver hair softly waved, she was small and frail-looking but elegant.

A butterfly fluttered in Kate's stomach.

"Ms. Lindstrom."

Kate swallowed and extended her hand. "Yes... I'm... I'm Katherine Lindstrom."

Brian flipped open his pocket-size notebook and scribbled down the license-plate number of a red Fiero. With a glance at his watch, he rushed back to his car to phone the office. "Brie, I've got the license number. I thought that the woman wasn't ever coming out of the house."

"Is she wife number two?"

"Yeah, I think so. The woman fit the description that we had. I'll give you the number. Would you check it? I have to—"

"Don't bother calling her," Sabrina said, interrupting him. "Kate called here."

"She did?"

"She went, Brian."

"To the Strantons'?"

"Yes. She asked if you'd pick her up."

Anxiety quickened the beat of his pulse. "What time?" As his sister answered, he glanced again at his watch. "I have to hurry. Can you handle everything there?"

"Go," Sabrina said. "You'd be useless to me here."

"Thanks."

"Brian."

"Yeah?"

"Good luck."

He needed it. He'd urged Kate to talk to Gertrude Stranton, but he was selfish enough to wish that she hadn't gone.

* * *

"I wasn't quite clear where to begin." Gertrude handed Kate a cup of tea.

She accepted it and took a sip without really tasting it.

"You're quite lovely."

Kate struggled to offer a polite smile. "Thank you."

"Yesterday morning, I told my husband about the letter from Mrs. Arneson. Douglas—"

Kate refused the sugar offered to her.

"My husband had to leave town on business and requested that I call you. I also told him about hiring Mr. Fleming."

Kate watched the woman's mouth. She spoke with extreme slowness, as if measuring each word.

"The letter came as such a shock to me. I couldn't ignore it." She lowered her head, then, as if she remembered who she was, she raised her face, and her blue eyes met Kate's again. "Douglas—we hope that you will try to understand."

"Understand what?"

"The circumstances that caused this situation."

Situation. She was a situation? Kate tightened her grip on the purse straps.

"We hope you won't feel too harshly toward any of us."

Kate couldn't stand it any longer. She'd waited too long, her whole life, to know. "Who is my father? You know, don't you?"

Brian drove his car through the gates and followed the winding driveway that led to the house, a two-story Georgian mansion with a second-story veranda.

He braked and turned off the ignition. As the windshield wipers stopped, snow blew against the windows. He huddled deeper in his jacket in response to the chill creeping into the car.

He'd sat outside a similar-looking house years ago, but the warmth of a summer sun had glared into his car then, and the scent of roses had filled his every breath with an almost nauseating sweetness. He'd waited nearly a half hour before Diane had finally joined him. He'd been younger then, a college kid eager for romance and passion. And impatient. Romance and passion were superficial reasons for why he was waiting now. Love gave a person no choices. For Kate, he'd wait forever.

"Please try to understand," Gertrude appealed. "Douglas had no choice."

With a Herculean effort, Kate kept her voice calm. The woman seemed insistent that she hear their feelings toward her. Kate cared about only one thing. "Am I your husband's daughter?"

Gertrude shook her head. "You're Edward's daughter."

Kate struggled to stay seated.

"But you must know—we want you to know... This is so difficult."

For me, too, Kate wanted to yell.

"Edward was young, and he succumbed to family pressure to marry the right woman, someone within our circle of friends, someone who could help a lawyer make his way into politics. He married Celeste Wendell. She was the perfect candidate for Edward's wife." The woman reached out to touch Kate's hand, but her fingers never made contact.

Why did such a painful moment have to be a part of anyone's life? Kate wondered.

"Celeste was quite lovely, and she loved Edward a great deal. I don't believe Edward ever felt the same depth of emotion for her, but their marriage wasn't unhappy. The future looked so bright for them, but tragedy..."

I should leave, Kate thought. She didn't want to know more. But as if glued to the spot, she didn't move.

"They'd been married several years when she had an accident. A terrible one." Gertrude Stranton's eyes remained steady on Kate's face, but her voice softened. "It left her paralyzed. She was twenty-five. Edward was only four years older. He met your mother. I don't really know how—what brought about their relationship. But he couldn't divorce Celeste."

As the older woman's head bowed slightly, Kate looked away, distressed by the woman's discomfort.

"Douglas told me that Edward truly loved your mother, but they knew that he could never leave Celeste." A sadness clouded the woman's soft blue eyes. "When Celeste's family learned about Edward and your mother, he was forced to stop seeing her. Douglas said that Edward was terribly lonely. And terribly desperate to see her again despite the risk."

"The risk to his political career?"

Setting down her teacup, Mrs. Stranton's hand trembled. "I'm sure that was a factor, but not entirely. Your mother had left the law firm and disappeared. Edward hired someone to locate her. It took a year. It was then he learned she'd died in a car accident. It was then that he learned about you. Douglas said that Edward never doubted you were his child. He trusted your mother. He loved her. But..." She looked pained. "Our family is ..."

Kate was beyond politeness. "He worried about scandal?"

"The media is so scrutinizing. If he had done anything about you, then everyone would have known."

Kate stiffened. "Yes, they would have."

"I'm sure he wanted to," she said quickly, "but he felt honor bound to protect Celeste from such public ridicule." She reached forward and touched Kate's hand. "We all do."

"She's been an invalid for nearly thirty years. She's in a nursing home now, but the family has to protect her. She did love him. She always talks about the days before her accident. You do see that he couldn't leave her after the accident, after he met your mother."

Kate drew a long breath. *She's telling me that I'm stronger.*

"She only has memories."

"I understand what you're saying," Kate cut in. She shouldn't have come, she thought. What had been gained? Nothing. "I'll go now."

"We'd like—"

Kate froze.

"We'd like very much if you would be a part of our family. We know we can't make up to you for all that you've suffered, Katherine, but..." She took a tremulous breath.

Numbed and speechless, Kate stared at her.

"We can't announce you as Edward's child." She managed a weak smile. "At least not now, not yet. You do understand that? But we want so much for you, one of our own, to share your life with us." The woman's voice cracked. "Would you allow that?"

Kate fought for calm against warring emotions. Resentment gave way beneath the power of suppressed childhood wishes. She succumbed to a yearning in her heart to belong, to be a part of a family, to be wanted. One word slipped out. "Yes."

Brian watched Kate's slender figure battle the wind during her dash toward his car. Head bent, she hid her face. He realized in that moment he needed to see her eyes. No matter what she told him, her eyes would reveal the truth.

A blast of cold wind accompanied her rush into the car. The dome light flashed for only a second. Brian peered at her in the car's dark interior.

"It wasn't what I expected," she said, smoothing the bottom of her coat.

Damp from the snow, her hair glistened. She shifted on the seat, facing him and relating the past few moments to him. He saw no tears. An underlying strength was evident in her voice. "I didn't want them to feel obligated now. Making someone do something means nothing."

"Is that what you think they're feeling?"

She shook her head while she looked down and straightened the knit scarf at her neck. "No, I don't. I'm glad I went. I learned that my parents loved each other. I was conceived in love, not wisely, but they did care deeply for each other. And I can't forget that he did support me."

He sensed that meant nothing to her.

"I'm trying to understand why the situation..." She closed her eyes for a second. "I wish—I wish just once he'd come to see me."

Brian draped an arm over the steering wheel and leaned toward her. As his hand closed over hers, she raised her eyes to him. Unhappiness still dulled them despite the smile she offered. "It's not easy, is it?"

"No," she admitted. "I keep wondering if they'd have ever bothered with me if Dorothy Arneson hadn't forced their hand."

"Kate, don't do that to yourself."

She pressed her lips together. "And I can't get past the hurt. I keep trying to. Now more than before."

"Because you know the truth?"

"Because they want me," she blurted out.

His grip tightened instinctively on her hand. *Be happy for her,* he demanded of himself, but he felt a growing tension grip his gut. "That's great."

She frowned. "Yes, it is. But..." She shifted to look at him.

"What?"

She shook her head as if banishing some thought. "Never mind."

"Kate?"

"Never mind."

He settled back behind the steering wheel. "I'll take you home."

"No!"

Brian frowned. "Where?"

She looked dumbfounded at her own outburst. "Not my place." She glanced at the house. Uncertainty etched faint lines in her face. "Take me to your home. I want to be with you tonight."

Chapter Ten

Honey..."

Kate unbuttoned her coat and tossed it onto the heavy cushioned tweed sofa in Brian's living room. "I don't want to talk about it. I really don't. I don't want to think about any of that."

As she walked toward him, Brian closed the door.

"Help me forget for a while."

She stood close against him and tugged off his coat. As her hand went to the buttons of his shirt, his heart thudded. He hadn't expected his own quick response, but he accepted the delight he felt at her closeness, the demand she effortlessly produced in him. Casually, she draped one arm over his shoulder while the fingers of her other hand unbuttoned his shirt. Tilting back her head, she looked up at him. He watched her lips part in an invitation.

"I know a great Swedish saying."

"In Swedish?"

"English."

"What is it?"

Her fingers slid across his chest. "Many hands make work light."

Brian smiled slowly.

"Hint, hint," she whispered against his ear.

He needed no suggestions. His fingers wound into her hair. His mouth captured hers. As the taste of her filled his mouth, he moved her backward toward the sofa. The warmth of her kiss, the caress of her hands, the meeting of their bodies drove him mad. But with a slowness, a pleasurable languid pace, they touched and tasted and aroused.

Darkness fell over the room. Moonlight pierced the blind. Shadows fell across her paleness and the angles of her body. He needed no light. He touched and molded her to him, gripping her tightly, fiercely, determined never to let her go.

"I heard music."

Kate smiled against his shoulder, and her lips grazed his flesh. "Did you? A drumroll?"

"Oh, yes."

"And cymbals?"

"Hmm."

The hardness of his body pressed against hers again. "Crescendos?"

"A chorus of hallelujahs." His mouth hovered near hers. "Let's see if we can put the symphony together again."

She nipped at his jaw. "You'll conduct?"

"My pleasure."

* * *

Winded from his morning run, Brian drew a long breath and flopped back against the refrigerator.

"I can't find a thing in this kitchen," Kate complained, standing on tiptoe and stretching to look into the top shelf of a kitchen cabinet.

"What are you looking for?" he asked between exaggerated breaths.

"Something that resembles a glass."

She whirled around to face him. Her hair tousled, she stood before him in his bathrobe, the sleeves rolled up to form bulky cuffs at her thin wrists. "I'm crazy about you," he said.

Her eyes swept over him. "I'm crazy about you."

He grinned at the shock that flashed across her face. "Surprised yourself, didn't you? The glasses are behind the pots."

She returned a soft smile. "How do you find anything?"

"I know where everything is."

"You have enough dishware and pots and pans here for three families."

"Two," he answered, slipping out of his jogging jacket. "Most of this stuff belonged to my parents. When Diane and I got divorced, I got the kitchenware."

She squatted down, disappearing from view.

He heard her rattling pots but left her alone. He'd been around her enough to know she was used to doing things for herself.

"And she got . . . ?"

"Everything she was used to having."

She popped up from behind the cabinet. "I found a glass."

As she poured juice into it, he volunteered, "I'll make breakfast."

"I was hoping you'd offer." She strolled toward the table and fingered his pocket-size notebook. "Are all your secrets in this little book?" Idly she toyed with a corner of the notebook.

"Talk about snoops."

She looked affronted. "I am not. I just wondered what you wrote in this. I saw it on the dashboard of your car when we drove to see Mrs. Arneson. What's in it?" she finally asked.

"Go ahead."

She flipped back the cover and frowned. "'He's throwing snowballs down the street'?" she read questioningly.

Brian pushed away from the refrigerator to pour himself coffee. He knew she'd turned a page as she continued reading.

"'To get the attention of a girl so sweet.' Brian, what is this?"

"A limerick. I write dumb limericks to pass the time when I'm doing surveillance work."

She gestured with her head toward the notebook. "Can I go ahead and thumb through it?"

"It's a new notebook. There isn't much in it."

Kate smiled at him then turned another page. "'She smiles at him with a cute little grin. He knows she's the girl he'd like to win.'" She giggled.

"I told you it's dumb."

"When did you write this?"

"While waiting for you during your meeting with Breshkov. By the way, when is your second audition?"

"Soon. Did this limerick just pop into your head?"

"I was watching a teenage kid. I could see that he was dying to make a pass at some girl across the street. Instead he threw a snowball at her."

"Typical move for an adolescent male." She turned another page.

"Maybe you should stop reading."

"This page is crossed out."

"Bad start." He moved toward her to grab the notebook.

She whirled around, offering him her back. "It's the same limerick. 'He's throwing snowballs down the street. To get the attention of a girl so sweet. He's much too old to play with a truck. What he'd rather do is...'" Slowly Kate looked over her shoulder at him. She shut the notebook and handed it to him. "I'll get dressed now."

Brian laughed as she hurried out of the room. "When I was a kid, I took one piano lesson. My aunt," he said loudly, reaching down for a frying pan, "refused to teach me."

"Why?" she yelled back.

"She detested swearwords."

"Piano teachers are very prim and proper ladies."

Brian thought about the previous night. "Lovely ladies," he replied. Prim and proper didn't quite fit, he reflected.

Stepping into her slacks, Kate scanned the bedroom lined with shelves of books. Law books dominated the space. Intermingled were a few science-fiction books and some autobiographies, one about a famous jazz musician who'd made a comeback after a courageous uphill climb from drug addiction.

Eclectic taste in everything, she decided, remembering the variety of music cassettes in his car.

"French toast okay?"

"Yes," Kate yelled back, dropping to her knees to hunt for her shoes. She reached under the bed. Instead of a shoe, her hand closed over a stack of paper. Kate pulled it out. Slowly, she smiled. "Do you remember when we talked about my teapot collection?"

"What?"

"My teapot collection," she said louder.

"What about it?"

"You said that you never collected anything." She looked up to see him standing in the doorway.

"Yeah, I said that."

Kate held the stack out toward him. "There must be hundreds of these under your bed. What do you call these?"

"*Spider-man* comic books."

"No," she insisted. "What do you call this?"

"Research."

She sat back on her heels and grinned at him. "For what?"

"Learning how to stretch from one rooftop to another."

"How long have you been collecting these?"

"I haven't been collecting them," he declared, but she saw laughter in his eyes.

"Of course not. They somehow piled up to a stack of two hundred?" she asked speculatively.

"Two hundred and twenty-one to be exact."

"Amazing."

"What is?"

"Your house being haunted by a ghost who leaves behind *Spider-man* comic books."

"I always thought so. Breakfast will be ready in a minute."

"I'm beginning to change my views about breakfast," Kate mumbled as she devoured her last piece of French toast.

"Glad to hear that. What else are you changing your mind about?"

She unclipped her watch and set it on the table, then pushed her chair back. Strolling toward the sink with her dish in her hand, she asked, "Is the detergent in this cabinet?"

Brian nodded in response to the direction she'd pointed. "On the left-hand side." He collected the dishes on the table while she ran water in the sink. "You can't avoid thinking about what happened yesterday evening, Kate."

"You're annoying."

"I've been told that before."

"Rolls right off you, doesn't it?"

"Don't get testy with me just because you don't want to talk about—"

"I'm not testy," she countered, interrupting him and plunging her hands into the suds. "Who else tells you that you're annoying?"

"My sister and I affectionately dance around each other to coexist."

She rinsed a plate. "Who's the difficult one?"

"She is."

Kate cocked an eyebrow.

He held his hands in the air in a framing gesture. "Me."

"You really didn't have to admit that."

"I had no choice. You have a wicked eyebrow."

She released a hearty laugh.

"Sometimes," he admitted, "you make me feel as if I've regressed to my first date."

Kate sent him a puzzled look.

"I said an amazing number of stupid things that day, too."

"I doubt that." She handed him another plate. "Did you like her a lot?"

"Yes. She laughed at everything I said, too."

"You're really not a typical private eye, Mr. Fleming."

"I'll buy a trench coat."

"You smile too much. What will you do about that?"

"Why do I have to do anything about it?"

"Private investigators are supposed to look glum. They're tough guys who constantly cast an evil eye at someone just for effect."

"You do like old movies, don't you?"

"Crazy about them."

"Kate, about last night—"

"And you don't own one mystery or detective story." She pulled the plug from the sink and watched the water swirl down the drain. "Why not?"

"I don't like to read them. I might learn that I don't know very much."

She felt his eyes studying her. When she faced him, he returned an unmistakably disapproving look. "Do you ever avoid anything?"

"I won't let you off the hook in this case."

"I'm—my world isn't the same anymore."

He led her toward the table and then gently pushed her onto the nearest chair.

"This isn't your business." She saw hurt in his eyes.

"You've known right from the beginning that I stick my nose into other people's business." His hand closed around hers. "Don't bottle it up inside you. You don't have to. I'm here. If you need someone to talk to, to lean on, lean on me."

She couldn't battle him and herself. "I'm being offered an opportunity to belong."

"It's what you've wanted."

"Is it?"

With a sigh, he touched her cheek.

"You're annoying again," she said.

He smiled weakly. "How?"

"You're too gentle, too compassionate."

"I'll punch you a few times."

She laughed then. It was a mistake. Letting go of one emotion at that moment released another. Her vision misted. Quickly Kate raised a hand and dabbed a finger at the corner of her eye. "Pride makes me want to reject what she offered. But she isn't at fault. The person who was is dead. He died, and I'll never know him. And I keep wondering if the time hasn't come for me to put the past to rest."

"It's what you want to do?"

"I told you last night what she said. They want me. But is it guilt making them say that?" She looked down for a second, then met his gaze again. "She asked me to stay last night."

His head snapped up. "What?"

"She asked me to stay."

"And you refused."

"Yes. I told her that I couldn't. That I had students coming for lessons."

He frowned. "What students?"

She shook her head. "I didn't have one last night. But so much was happening. I couldn't stay there. And I couldn't go home. I didn't know where I belonged." Raw emotion overwhelmed her. "I'm doing what I enjoy now. I have a life of my own, a career, friends," she rushed on. She pressed her fingers tighter on his. "Some very important ones."

"So what have you decided?"

"No advice?"

"I'm offering support, not answers."

She curled a hand around his neck. He offered so much more than she'd ever known before, ever expected. "I'm going tonight."

He simply nodded, registering no expression.

"And—and she told me that they're having a party Friday night." As his eyebrows drew together, she added quickly, "This Friday. The banquet is on the following Saturday, isn't it?"

"Yes."

"I was sure it was. Gertrude's husband—"

"Douglas?"

"Yes. Douglas. He'll be back then from his business trip. I need to talk to him. He knew everything, Brian. He paid Dorothy Arneson for my fath—for his brother. He..." She felt her anger stirring again. "I want to meet him."

"And then?"

Kate inclined her head. "And then what?"

"What happens after that?"

"I'm not thinking beyond the next day and then the one after that. But I'd like you to go with me Friday night."

He started to shake his head.

"You were willing before. You offered before to go with me."

"You did all right alone."

"I don't want to be alone on Friday evening."

He pulled his hand from hers. "I don't own a tux."

"Couldn't you rent one?"

"No!" He pushed himself to his feet.

Bewildered, Kate stared at the empty chair for a long second. The bang of a cupboard door behind her made her whirl around. "Why are you angry at me?"

"Not at you. Me." He jammed his hands into his jeans pockets. "Ghosts of the past," he answered.

"Is this a riddle?" she demanded.

"No riddle."

"Does their money bother you?"

His body straightened from its relaxed pose. "Hell, no! Why would you think that?"

Her eyes shifted to an oversize bottle on top of the refrigerator. "I save keepsakes from students. You save pennies."

"That makes me a reverse snob?"

"No, but you've said things about Diane, about her family that—"

"Their money wasn't important to me, just to them."

"But the wealth bothered you?"

"The way they acted because of that wealth bothered me, Kate."

She truly didn't understand his reluctance to go with her.

"I didn't like their life-style. Or what it did to Diane."

Kate looked away. *Lean on me,* he'd said. But he hadn't meant those words. Not really. Disappointment churned up anger again. "You push and you push, but you don't like it when someone does it back, do you?"

"No, I don't."

"So you won't go with me." She ran her hand through the air. "Fine. I'll ask someone else."

He crossed the room in two strides. "What did you say?"

Kate saw anger in his eyes. She realized that she'd never seen it before in him. Her chin went up as she made an effort to meet his gaze head-on. "I'll ask someone else."

"Like hell you will."

"That's right. I will. Did you think that you're the only man I know?"

"I thought that I was the only one lately."

"Did you?"

"Don't be coy."

"Coy? Is that what I'm being?" she asked dumbly, circling to the opposite side of the table.

He released a mirthless, almost silent laugh. "Damn, but you keep me guessing more than any woman I've ever known," he said half to himself.

He was playing it light, Kate realized gratefully. Her reaction to his refusal had been childish. If he'd stayed angry, they'd both have said words, stupid words to each other. Why had she tried such an adolescent move on him? She'd never done that before with any man. Why with him? She wanted him with her. She needed him with her. For the first time in her adult life, she was facing something that might be easier if she wasn't alone. But she didn't want to feel that way. And acting coy or deliberately stirring up jealousy wasn't her style. "You're the only one," she said softly.

A slow smile spread across his face as he settled on a chair. "Then I guess I'm the one who should be by your side Friday."

"You'll go?"

"Why so surprised?"

"Because I knew that you weren't fooled by what I'd said about someone else."

"Once I dug the green-eyed monster's claws out of my back, I wasn't."

"I apologize. In fact, I'll make dinner tonight to make up for it."

"Tonight you're busy."

Kate frowned, realizing she'd forgotten her promise to Gertrude. "Yes, I am. Tomorrow night, then."

He toyed with her watch. "Something that isn't green?"

"Promise."

"Your watch is slow." Brian dangled the watch by its plain black band.

"Is it really?"

"Look for yourself."

Kate strolled around the table to stand beside him. She looked over his shoulder at the watch. Her eyes darted from the plain oval face to the clock on the stove. "You're crazy."

He yanked her down to his lap. "About you."

Kate coiled her arms around his neck. "My watch has the same time as your clock."

"So it does," he said, not even bothering to compare the time on them. He leaned forward to put the watch on the table and brushed his lips against her collarbone.

"You're a sneak."

"We've discussed this before."

"Repeatedly," she agreed. "And you always verify it by doing another sneaky thing."

"What did I do this time?"

"Got me over here on false pretenses."

"I'd never do that. I knew exactly what I was getting you over here for. You're the one who didn't know."

"It's still snowing."

"You're not cooperating," he grumbled as she stretched away from him to look out the window. "It's a good day for staying inside."

"Or a great day for having fun."

"That's what I had in mind."

"This isn't what I had in mind, Kate," Brian muttered, packing snow on an already paunchy snowman.

She eyed his creation. "You make a lousy snowman. He's got a pin head."

"You build yours. I'll build mine."

"I'm almost done." She bent over and rolled the oblong lump of snow.

"Hey, Picasso."

"You're speaking to me, I assume?" Bent over, she looked back at him. "Now what's wrong with my figure?" she asked in advance.

He gave her a wicked grin, his eyes fixing on her backside. "Not a thing. But are you building a snowman or a snowwoman?"

"Snowman. Why?"

"Because your snowman looks pregnant."

Kate straightened and studied it. "I give up."

"I thought you'd never say that."

"You're right. We should go in." She brushed her snow-covered mittens together.

"Finally." He stepped back to admire his snowman. Kate expected him to drop to all fours in the manner of a golfer lining up his putt. "Do you play golf?"

"Not in winter. So don't ask."

"Did you think I was going to?"

"I'm never sure what you'll suggest."

"Come inside," she said, smiling. "I'll tell you."

His eyes danced. "That's what I had in mind all along."

"Compatibility has merit."

"Who said it didn't?" he asked, packing more snow against the misshapened statue.

Kate stood behind him and tilted her head. "He has no fanny."

Brian scooped up another handful of snow.

"Did you think we were all along?"

"Compatible?"

"Yes." Kate frowned. "You are going to fix his head, aren't you?"

"His head is fine."

She stared doubtfully at the snowman. "Well, you do hate green food."

"No, I don't. I like asparagus."

"You thought my teapot collection was silly."

"Did I ever say that?"

"You gave me a look."

"What look?"

"That look you get when you're having trouble understanding something."

"When else did I give you that look?"

Kate reached for the baseball cap that they'd brought outside with them. "When I told you to leave before Estelle came in."

"That's because I didn't know it was Estelle who was at your door. The woman drove me crazy while I was married to Diane. She'd—"

Kate handed him the cap. "It won't fit."

"It will."

"What did Estelle do?"

"She's a class-A busybody."

Kate smiled at the expression.

"And that's a kind description of her. She was a good friend of my ex-mother-in-law's and felt it was her responsibility to keep an eye on Diane, since she lived in the same city with us and my in-laws were spending most of their time at Lake Tahoe." Brian plunked the hat onto the snowman's head. It dropped down to cover three-quarters of the face. "Don't say it," he warned.

Kate smiled at his back. "Say what?"

"I told you so."

"Would I do that?"

"It's one of your famous looks."

She stepped around him and tilted the baseball hat back so she could shove two enormous buttons onto the snowman's face. "Do I have other endearing looks?"

"One."

Kate reached into her jacket pocket for a wedge of carrot.

"A very endearing one," he said, scooping her up into his arms.

Kate laughed. "Should I guess which one?"

"I'd rather just see it again," he said, carrying her toward the back stairs of the house.

"We didn't finish the snowman."

"He's finished."

Kate glanced back at him. "He certainly is," she said on a giggle, and dropped the carrot in the snow.

Chapter Eleven

Kate refused to fidget as she sat down at a table that could accommodate twenty. Only two settings of Haviland china and Waterford crystal adorned the long table. Only hers and Gertrude's voices filled the room through seven courses. They shared a history of their lives, and though the woman was easy to talk to, Kate felt the evening's emotional strain. By the time she was shown to the guest bedroom, she was exhausted.

Sprawled across the bed, she looked about the room. An antique dealer's dream of heaven. She stared at her reflection in an ornate Chippendale mirror with a gilt edge. The faint scent of lemon oil lingered in the air.

Kate closed her eyes, but a vision of Brian, more real than her surroundings, came to mind. She stretched toward the edge of the bed, reaching for the telephone on the nightstand.

Brian slouched lower on the oatmeal-colored sofa and yawned. He closed his eyes and blocked out the corny dialogue of a 1950s Western movie blasting from the television set. He heard instead Kate's low husky laugh, her girlish giggle, her soft whispers. He was torturing himself, he decided, and felt relieved at the grating shrill of the telephone.

It rang only once before he grabbed the receiver.

"Brian?"

He sprang forward. "What's wrong?"

"Nothing."

"Are you at the Strantons'?"

"Yes."

"Are you alone?"

"I'm in the guest bedroom. It's bigger than my apartment."

He cradled the phone closer. "An exaggeration."

"Only slightly. I wish I were with you."

Instant pleasure surged through him. "I miss you." He slouched again and closed his eyes, letting the softness of her voice drift over him.

"I'll be home by noon tomorrow. In the morning I have to shop for a dress."

"For the big event?"

"What big event?"

"Your debut."

"No, it isn't that. I told you that they can't tell anyone."

"You're still agreeing to that?"

"It's the only thing that I really do understand. I see no point in hurting Celeste Stranton. She's an innocent party. If she needs to believe that her husband was faithful throughout their marriage, I'm not going to be responsible for taking that from her."

"So what is the party for?"

"Gertrude belongs to a committee for the performing arts. It's a celebration party Friday night for the fund-raisers."

"What is their story going to be about you?"

"That I'm a relative, one of those cousins they didn't realize they had."

"I wouldn't believe it."

Her voice lightened. "That's because you're the man who makes a habit of reading between the lines." She sighed softly. "It's been an odd evening. Someone came to the door. Instead of a buzzer, they have soft chimes."

"You can't seriously be missing that buzzer?"

Kate laughed.

"Are you going to sleep now?"

"Uh-huh."

He inhaled deeply. The fragrance of her perfume lingered in the air of his living room as if she'd staked a claim there. "I'll be thinking of you. Complete with mental images. But it won't be the same as having you here."

He heard a giggle in her voice. "I hope not. Before you go, let me give you the name and address of a man who has a combo."

Brian leaned forward and rummaged through the coffee-table drawer for a pencil. "What's it consist of?"

"Cello, piano, and drums. Sometimes a guitarist. Burly Mead is the man in charge."

"Who?"

"That's his name."

"You don't believe that?"

"Of course, not. His real name is Bertram. But that's not jivey enough."

"I'll talk to him tomorrow," he said, scribbling the address across a sheet of paper.

"Did you think that I'd let you down?"

Never. "Not me."

"Good night."

"Sleep well, Kate." He heard the click and reached forward to set down the receiver. "I love you," he said, feeling as if more than distance was suddenly between them.

"I have to tell you, Katie," Liz whispered the next morning as she eyed a glittering black gown, "I wouldn't have had the nerve to step into this shop."

Kate peeked around a red sequined dress at her. "Why?"

"It's too rich for my blood. Blame it on those crazy sweatshirts that you always wear, but I didn't know you shopped at places like this."

"I normally don't."

"This shop makes Saks look like a bargain basement."

"This isn't quite that exclusive," Kate responded.

"How does a piano teacher afford clothes at these prices?"

"What prices?" Kate whispered back. "Nothing is tagged."

"Didn't you know that?"

"No, someone suggested this shop to me."

"May I help you," a feminine voice said from behind Kate.

* * *

"Hey, man, sure I can help you."

Brian took a cautious step into Burly Mead's apartment. It contained a piano, a set of drums, a cello and an army cot. Burly had a smooth young face and deep-set green eyes. A thin, tall man, Burly looked like a Bertram. "Kate Lindstrom—"

"Super lady."

Brian tucked his tongue in his cheek.

"Your lady, right?"

Brian grinned. "She told me that you're a good musician."

"The best." He puffed his chest slightly. "Don't let the pad throw you."

"I'm not." Brian glanced at the baby grand piano. "Everybody has their own priorities."

The young man swung his hands together in an eager clap. "So, what can I do for you?"

"I'd like your combo to play at a banquet."

"When's the gig? We're lined up pretty tight."

Brian played along with him. "Yeah, I guess you would be. A week from Saturday."

"Hmm." He whirled around and faced a calendar that was tacked to the wall.

Though his back blocked the view, Brian had noticed the calendar when he'd walked in. It was one that insurance companies gave to customers. Only three notations had been scribbled on it.

Burly made a pretense of running a finger along calendar dates in a pondering manner. "Looks good," he said brightly.

"Can I hear your group first?"

"Let me ring them up."

Brian glanced at his watch. "I don't have a lot of time."

"You aren't going to need much, man. One song, and you'll know we're exactly what you want."

"It was exactly what I wanted, but—"

Liz gripped Kate's arm in a conspiratorial manner as they crossed the street. "Expensive," Liz responded, drawing out the word for emphasis.

"What did I ask for?" Kate reminded her.

"Something formal."

"And simple." She sent Liz a quick grin. "And reasonably priced," Kate added, laughing.

"That it isn't."

"But it is beautiful."

"That it is. So you starve for a while."

Kate's smile slipped. She nodded in response to Liz's comment, her thoughts returning to the salesclerk in the boutique. She'd maintained a plastic smile until Kate had dug into her purse for her checkbook.

The woman had frowned instantly. "This has been taken care of," she'd informed Kate in her perfectly modulated voice. "Mrs. Stranton called and informed me that you might visit our boutique."

Kate had fought a panicked sensation, feeling as if she was losing control of her own life. She'd regained it quickly, insisting, "I'll pay for the dress."

"Do you have time for lunch?" Liz asked now, forcing Kate to focus on her surroundings.

Kate glanced at the unfamiliar watch on her wrist and frowned. "Yes. A hamburger."

Liz tugged at her arm. "I know a cheap place."

"I don't smell anything cooking." Brian sniffed as he slipped off his coat.

As he headed for her kitchen, Kate blocked his path. "Don't be so nosy."

"But nothing is cooking," he said, stretching first to one side and then the other to look around her for the sight of a pot or a pan on the stove.

She framed his face with her hands and kissed him. "I promised you dinner, didn't I?"

"Yeah, you did."

"Then I'll give you dinner."

He pulled her closer.

"Until then, why don't we play cards for a while?"

"Cards?"

She slipped out of his arms.

"Surely we could think of something else to do."

Turning to face him, she held up a deck of cards. "A game of gin?"

He couldn't resist the impish face tilted up at him. He covered her lips with a longer, more lingering kiss. As he released her, she sighed, fanning his face with her warm breath. "Do you feel like losing?"

She ran a finger down his neck to the base of his throat. "Still haven't learned, have you?"

"I'll let you win the first two hands," he said as he grabbed her wrist and then kissed a fingertip.

Kate pulled back and ducked under his arms. "Good. I'll beat you silly then."

He clicked his tongue. "Such modest charm."

Kate curtsied slightly. "Thank you."

"Let's hope you're also a gracious loser," he quipped, passing by her and lightly swatting her backside. "I have always had a lucky streak."

"Have you?"

"Found you, didn't I?"

She won the first five out of six hands. As she fingered and then slowly lifted the two of spades from the deck of discards, he recognized that tossing away that two to keep her from getting three of a kind had turned on him.

"Gin," she sang out proudly, setting down a run, including his two.

He frowned. "You're just plain lucky."

"Right."

He tossed his cards down on the coffee table. "Deal."

Though she pulled a straight face, she struggled to stifle a smile. As she bent forward and dealt the hand, strands of hair brushed her cheek. He touched them, watching the light shine on them as he let them slip through his fingers.

"Cards?" she insisted.

Her eyes sparkled at him. He was tempted to toss the cards into a corner of the room.

"Pick up your hand," she taunted. "Or do you concede the game?"

Brian snatched up his cards. He had to win a hand first. But how? he wondered as he stared at the mismatched hodgepodge of suits that she'd dealt him.

"Last night was odd—and long," she said, then grinned. "You don't have a poker face."

He narrowed his eyes at her. "Better?"

She shook her head, smiling. "No."

"So, why was it a long night?"

She outlined his bottom lip with a finger. "I missed you."

He raised his head and then leaned across the coffee table to press his forehead to hers. He insisted on eye contact. "You cheat."

"I don't."

"You're taking advantage of my madness for you."

She pulled back on a giggle. "Play the game."

"So what happened last night?"

"I wanted a cup of coffee," she said, staring at the cards fanned out in her hand.

He shoved an ace beside another one and reached down for his next card while he gave her a knowing look.

"I started to go down the stairs to the kitchen. It seemed easier than calling the maid, who'd have to climb the stairs then go back down to inform the cook about what I wanted."

"Gertrude Stranton stopped you?"

Kate met his eyes. "Yes. She explained that if I got the coffee myself, I'd make the maid and the cook feel unimportant and insecure in their jobs."

"It's difficult to remember that, isn't it?"

"When you were married to Diane, did you feel the same thing?"

"The only time I felt that was when we visited her family. And that wasn't often. But when you're used to doing things yourself, it's a rude awakening to realize not everyone does."

"I had trouble with the chain of command," she admitted.

"There are definite rules to follow."

"I've noticed."

"Expect more of them."

Kate stared at her cards. "I'm only going to that party tomorrow and—"

He grimaced.

"Don't made a face. It won't be so bad."

"I didn't make it because of that. I'm starving."

"Be patient a few minutes more. Concentrate on the cards." A corner of her lips tugged upward in a teasing grin. "What happened to that lucky streak of yours."

"You stole it."

"It's not luck for me. It's skill," Kate taunted lightly.

"Lucky enough." He glanced up again, but the glint of gold on her wrist distracted him from smiling at her. "Nice watch."

Her eyes lowered. "Gertrude gave it to me. She wants me to call her aunt—in private."

Brian remained silent.

"I can't."

"Why not?"

"It doesn't feel right."

"What does?"

She leaned across the table and kissed him. "You."

"Puns now?"

"To distract you," she admitted unabashedly. "I think you're going to win this hand," she added, frowning at her cards.

"A miracle. If I get one, maybe I'll get another. Like dinner?" he prodded.

"Dinner—" Kate stopped in response to the buzzer. "Good." She pushed herself out of the chair. "I was afraid you'd start snarling soon. Your stomach controls your mood." She shot a grin back at him as she strolled toward the door.

"It does not."

"Ha!" She swung open the door to allow the entrance of a white-jacketed waiter. He pushed a linen-draped cart. The scent of flowers entered the room along with the lilting strains of a violinist.

Brian shoved the cards together in a stack and then pushed himself to his feet. "Are you romancing me?"

She returned his smile. "I couldn't possibly have cooked for you," she whispered, standing close to him.

"Why not?"

"I might never have seen you again."

Brian dropped his napkin onto the plate and reached for the glass of champagne.

"Delicious, wasn't it?"

"Yes." He peered over the rim of the glass at her. "Did you choose the menu?"

"Actually, no."

He gestured with his hand. "Was this your idea?"

"No, again. Gertrude asked me to stay for dinner tonight. I told her that I had other plans." Kate saw no smile in his eyes and felt muscles tense at the back of her neck. "I mentioned that I'd promised dinner to you. She suggested this caterer. You didn't like it?"

"Not your average take-out place."

"What's wrong with this?"

He leaned forward and set the glass on the table. "I'm a man with simple tastes. I like spaghetti and red wine and music from the stereo. If it had been your idea, I'd be thrilled."

Her tense muscles started to burn.

"Maybe it's right for you. But it's not for me, Kate. I've done this before. It didn't work out."

The tension remained with Kate the following evening. As a uniformed maid ushered them toward French doors in the Strantons' home, Kate felt pulled in two different directions.

Opened, the doors led into a room gleaming beneath several crystal chandeliers and jammed with men in tuxedos and women in glimmering gowns.

"The next political pawn," Brian said low, directing Kate's gaze to the carefully groomed fair-haired man who'd attracted a substantial audience.

Though the buzz of conversation and sporadic, subdued laughter filled the room, the soft tones of a piano grabbed her attention. She nodded in response to Brian's comment, but eyed the Steinway. The pianist played Gershwin, but she heard Tchaikovsky in her mind, his Concerto in B-flat Minor.

"Kate?"

She slid her hand into his.

"You were swaying," he whispered.

"No, I was playing Tchaikovsky on a Steinway." Self-consciously she glanced around.

Brian touched her bare shoulders. "Easy."

She took an exaggeratingly long breath. "I'm trying."

He grabbed two champagne glasses from a tray on the table beside him. "Here." He handed one thin-stemmed glass to her. "We can't have you wringing your hands."

"I've never wrung my hands."

"Good. Let's keep it that way."

Kate nodded, but fingered the skirt of her soft, flowing white gown while she battled nervousness.

He gave her an appreciative look, his eyes sweeping down the cloth that covered one shoulder and draped around her breasts and hips. "You look like a Renaissance angel."

"I believe you have a poet's soul."

He laughed. "You know me better than that."

"I know you well enough to say that," she countered.

"Katherine!" A woman's high-pitched voice intruded on their privacy.

Brian straightened his back as Estelle Manington approached. She waddled toward them in a bright rose-colored gown that made her look like a plump tulip. Arms outstretched, she offered Kate the obligatory social greeting and grazed her powdered cheek across Kate's. "I was quite astounded when I saw you here. However, Gertrude explained that you weren't performing, as I'd assumed. A relative of hers?" she said on a note more disbelieving than questioning. "Why didn't you ever tell me?"

Beneath his hand, Brian felt Kate tense. He took a protective step forward, forcing Estelle to notice him.

Her heavily mascaraed eyes darted to his face. "Brian? Brian, is it really you?"

He shoved a hand into his pants pocket. "Estelle."

"My goodness, it's been an incredibly long time. Several years since we've seen each other."

"Yes, a long time," he said to keep conversation flowing.

"And now..." Her eyes darted back to Kate. "I've seen you twice in less than three weeks." Speculatively she peered over jeweled glasses at Kate.

"My investigative agency is near Kate's home," Brian went on, demanding her attention to end the woman's inquisitive look at Kate. "My sister took piano lessons. Did you every meet my sister?"

The woman shook her head, a confused expression knitting her forehead.

"Sabrina," he said, continuing to fill the conversation with inconsequential comments.

"And Katherine..." Estelle's eyes widened with comprehension. "Yes, I see how you met now. You gave his sister piano lessons." She chattered on. Narcissistic, she failed to notice Kate's discreet roll of her eyes at Brian.

Brian maintained a polite pose, but his gaze surveyed the room. A few familiar faces caught his eye, but he saw no one he wanted to talk to. Looking down while Estelle bent Kate's ear about her daughter, Brian watched feet shuffle. He noted polite shifts from one conversation to another just by observing the movement of feet. A familiar expensive scent made him look up to scan the sea of faces.

"Do you see anyone you know?"

He looked down at Kate. "When did Estelle depart?"

"A second ago. She said ta-ta."

"Ta-ta to her, too."

Kate giggled.

She was nervous, he realized, and he longed for the sound of the low, husky laugh that made his toes curl. He slid his hand across her back. The soft material of her gown slithered against his palm, bringing to mind a softer texture beneath it. He had never believed in romantic nonsense, but now he knew a man could get intoxicated just from the sight of something beautiful. Staring at her hair swept up and piled on her head, he reined in an erotic image. Later he'd slowly pull the pins from her hair and watch it tumble to her shoulders.

Kate discreetly pushed her hip against his. "You lied to Estelle about your sister."

"By omission. But she's a barracuda. She wanted me to admit that I picked you up."

"You didn't."

"Would you rather I'd told her how we'd really met?"

A tendril of hair brushed her neck as she shook her head. "No, that wouldn't have been a good idea."

With the movement of her head, he ached to kiss the curve of her neck. That probably wouldn't be a good idea, either, he decided without too much thought.

"Brian?" A round man with shiny cheeks and a receding hairline rushed toward them. Vigorously he pumped Brian's hand. "We haven't see you in—in..."

"A long time."

"Congratulations on your success with the Donner investigation."

"How did you hear about that?"

"Your name was mentioned in the newspaper as the investigator who aided the police."

Brian managed a strained smile.

"Lydia and I have recommended you to anyone who's in need of such service."

With his peripheral vision, Brian noticed Kate's gaze shifting toward Gertrude.

"How many of the paintings were finally recovered? The newspaper article stated six."

"Seven."

"Wonderful. And wonderful seeing you again." The man nodded politely at Kate and drifted toward the buffet table, stopping every few steps to greet someone.

Nothing had changed, Brian thought. The man still sprinkled his conversation with the word *wonderful*.

"Quite a hero."

Brian dismissed her remark with a shrug. Concern about the worried look on her face seemed more important. "It pays to read *Spider-man*."

She leaned forward as if to see his face better. "What are you doing?"

"Observing." He slipped an arm around her shoulder. "The woman in the pink burlap dress doesn't believe a thing she's hearing."

"That's not burlap."

"Whatever. She doesn't believe what she's hearing."

"Are you a psychic suddenly?"

"No," he said low, as if telling her a government secret. "But her head is back in a lofty pose."

Discreetly Kate nudged him with her elbow. "If you look around the room, you'll see several people in that pose."

"You are at a blue-blood function. No pedestrian ways here."

"What's the difference between the pink lady and the blond Ken who's stuffing shrimp in his mouth?"

"The blonde had a soporific droop of the eyelids, arching brows."

Laughter crept into her voice. "What's he saying?"

"Everything is repugnant."

Kate sipped her champagne. "Ah, the shrimp tastes foul."

"No, other people are repugnant. He thinks that he's above the others."

"Well, he is a tall man."

He sent her a psuedo-threatening look. "Denseness doesn't suit you."

"So everyone has a phony smile, then?"

He touched a fingertip to her smiling lips. "Not everyone."

"I've decided that your quirks are what I like best about you."

He grinned broadly, pleased she'd responded with a tease, and began looking for another candidate to discuss.

"Who are you staring at now?"

"My Aunt Ethel."

"Your aunt is here?"

"No, the woman looks like my aunt. The piano teacher," he added as explanation.

"Which one? I want to know what a prim-and-proper lady who detests swearwords looks like."

"Over there." He indicated a thin, sour-looking woman.

Kate responded with a feigned shudder. "No wonder you gave up piano lessons."

"She was terribly absentminded."

"Was she?"

He noted Kate's fingers still clutching the stem of the champagne glass in a death grip and went on, "I remember one day in particular. It started raining right after her friend left the house, so she ran after the friend to offer her an umbrella. She chased after this friend for two blocks. The friend declined the umbrella because she was nice and dry. She was wearing a raincoat."

"And?"

"And Aunt Ethel, satisfied that her friend wouldn't get wet, closed the umbrella, and then hurried home."

"She forgot to open the umbrella to keep herself dry?"

"She was soaked when she got home."

Kate smiled with delight. "Thank you."

"For what?"

"Your ridiculous story. I'm not nearly as nervous as I was when we walked in here. That was your plan, wasn't it?"

"It worked?"

"You have an amazing knack for making me smile at the silliest things."

As she leaned closer, heat radiated through him. "My aunt is really a lovely lady," he assured her, "but she was an old maid for a long time."

Kate wrinkled her nose. "Lousy term."

"She was one. She married for the first time at fifty-five."

Her eyes brightened. "Did she really?"

"Yeah, she did. To an old gentleman who lived down the street from her whom she'd known for thirty-five years. One day they really looked at each other." He brushed his lips across her cheek. "And it was magic."

A distinct clearing of a throat broke them apart. Kate smiled uneasily at Gertrude, but it was the man standing beside her who caught her attention.

Though elderly, he stood ramrod straight, and looked aggressively fit. His silver hair crowned a face with taut features and penetrating dark blue eyes.

Gertrude held his arm proprietorially. "Katherine, I'd like you to meet my husband, Douglas."

His eyes skimmed her with the arrogance of power.

Kate returned a steady, studying stare. His face wasn't unfamiliar to her.

"Mr. Fleming, we've met before." Douglas Stranton cocked his silver head. "Years ago?"

Brian extended a hand. "Several times."

Gertrude visibly squeezed her husband's arm. "At the Van Hammons'."

The briefest flicker of a question flashed across her husband's face, then recognition replaced it. "Yes, I remember now. Katherine, may I have a few words alone with you," he requested.

She took a deep breath, no longer feeling the sparkle of champagne or the humor of Brian's words clinging to her. "Yes," she said, accepting the arm that he offered her.

"Mr. Fleming." Kate heard Gertrude's voice. Crisp but not clipped, it contained a command. "Would you escort me back to Senator Daniels?"

Shaky, Kate let herself be led toward the double doors at the end of a long hallway. Propriety and confusion battled each other. She moved like a zombie. What she wanted to do was demand why the man beside her had lacked the decency to contact her.

She preceded him into the room and whirled around.

Lighting a pipe, he grinned up at her almost apologetically. "I hope you don't mind if I smoke. Gertrude nags me constantly about it, so for her sake, I never do so in her presence. Do you mind?"

Kate's anger ebbed. "Not at all," she murmured, aware now that she'd seen him before. She breathed deeply, taking in the scent of a familiar tobacco.

Chapter Twelve

The expensive fragrance caught Brian's attention again. The woman wearing it stood near the blond man with the ravenous appetite for shrimp. They were a matching set of elegance. Her pale hair flowed over her shoulders but failed to hide the intricate silver filigree that adorned her neck. She held a glass of Perrier in one hand and brushed the cheek of her companion with her other. He returned a token affection, placing a light hand on her back as if concerned with damaging the glittery silver sheath she wore.

Brian strolled toward the hallway. He bumped shoulders with another man and excused himself. The man never missed a beat in his conversation.

"More than one congressional district is at stake," he said to his companion.

Brian kept walking, catching bits and pieces of conversation.

"Her purple anemones were beautiful last summer," one woman chirped.

"She has a quaint little garden," another woman drawled.

Brian maneuvered himself toward a far end of the room.

"They bought a house."

"East Hampton, I understand."

"Yes, they're divorcing before escrow even closes."

After all these years, nothing had changed, not even the conversations, he reflected. His collar felt tight, and he squirmed against the restraint. Standing at the edge of the room, he glanced down the hall toward the double doors. *My thoughts are with you, Kate.*

"I *have* seen you before," Kate insisted.

"Shall we sit down?" Douglas suggested.

Kate remained standing. "At the children's home." Her eyes fixed on his pipe. "I remember your tobacco."

"Yes, I was there often—watching you."

Kate pressed her leg against the sofa behind her and reached down to steady herself as she sat.

"I had to be discreet," he said, sitting beside her. "The press hounds people in our position." His eyes looked sad; the blue in them softened. "But we always knew what was happening to you. You do understand why we couldn't . . . ?"

"Public scrutiny."

"He was a politician." Douglas Stranton maintained his proud posture, but his voice was less commanding. "I can't make excuses for him or myself to you. His political career was very important to him. Our whole family was always under a microscope, but

I—we managed to keep in touch with Mrs. Arneson to learn what you were doing and what you wanted.''

Kate held her breath for a second.

"My wife and I never had a child.'' His voice softened to a whisper. "I always thought of you as mine, the one Gertrude and I never had. For a short time I considered telling Gertrude and adopting you, but we weren't young, and the media allows us no privacy. I had to consider that the truth might be revealed. I couldn't risk ruining his career. And there was Celeste to think about. She was our sole concern. Even today, she must come first in our minds.''

Kate wrapped her arms across her chest.

His voice cracked noticeably. "I held you,'' he said, avoiding her eyes.

"You held me?''

"Oh, yes. Only once. You were very small. But from that day on...'' He raised his eyes to her, but Kate saw uncertainty. "You had my heart,'' he said finally. "I loved you as if you were my own.''

Tears burned her eyes. She placed her hands in her lap, clenching them tightly.

In a tentative manner, his gnarled hand touched, then closed over hers. "Please, understand. He loved your mother. He loved her desperately.''

Ghosts of the past haunted him, Brian had said once. Her, too, she realized. It was time to put them to rest. Once and for all. She stared into Douglas Stranton's eyes glazed with unshed tears. "Yes,'' she said simply, softly.

His shoulders raised as if a weight had been lifted from them. "May I ask one favor?''

Her lips trembled when she attempted a weak smile. "Of course.''

"Would you let an old man hold you once more?"

They came together stiffly, awkwardly, then his embrace tightened. Kate closed her eyes as she felt his tear against her cheek. They remained still, neither tightening nor lessening the pressure of the embrace. Years returned to her, years when she'd shed tears because no one had wanted her, no one had cared about her. And yet someone had been near. Someone had cared. Someone had shed tears with her.

A hand gripped Brian's shoulder. He controlled a reflex to turn around swinging, but his fist remained clenched when he faced the man who'd clamped his fingers on his shoulder.

"Trish said that she'd seen you," said a thin man with a nasal voice. He lit a cigarette with a slim gold lighter. Studying the ember on his cigarette in the way a young child fixes his gaze on an ant, he continued, "I didn't believe her. But here you are."

"Yes, here I am."

"You look good—no, better than good."

Brian met his gaze. "Good," he mimicked. "Still speculating in the stock market, Mitch?"

"As a hobby."

"And when you're not?"

"I have several other interests."

Brian maintained a fixed expression, but he wished the party were over. Too many people, he thought as he remembered similar endless parties while married to Diane.

With his peripheral vision, he caught sight of Kate entering the room. Her arm was hooked with Douglas Stranton's. She'd accepted him, he guessed. That was for the best.

"Circulate," Mitch suggested. "You might meet some new people." A high-pitched, phony laugh slipped from his throat. "And some old acquaintances."

Brian glared at him. He wanted to lower the man's nose several inches—preferably with his fist.

Kate skirted around two couples in an intense discussion about foreign policy.

She sidled up to Brian. "Who was the gentleman you were talking to?"

He ignored her question. "Am I glad to see you."

She smiled. "Missed me?"

"Unbelievably. Did it go well?"

"Very well. I buried old ghosts."

"I wish that I could say the same." He slid an arm around her waist, needing the contact. "Why don't we see what there is to eat?"

Kate frowned at the group gathered around the buffet table. "Too crowded."

"I'll bring you back something."

"Katherine," Estelle cooed.

Kate gripped his arm. "Don't go," she said through barely moving lips.

"You jest."

She tightened her fingers on his arm and sucked in air before facing Estelle.

"Gertrude told me that they were hoping to convince you to open a studio. I do hope so. I really found it extremely discomforting to bring Lisa to that tacky apartment building."

Concentrating more on Brian easing his arm free from her fingers, she ignored Estelle's comment.

"Not that it isn't lovely for what it is. But you should be a teacher in surroundings more befitting your background."

"My background?"

"You are a relative of the Strantons. Even a distant one is obligated to present the right impression. Don't you agree, Brian?"

"Excuse me, ladies." His eyes danced with suppressed humor. "I'll get you some food, Kate."

Estelle tipped her head toward Kate's. "Katherine, I'm so glad to get you alone. I'm hostessing a small informal party for Trey Dossin and his new wife. You must come. Anyone who is anyone will be there."

She took a step to the side, her bulky frame forcing Kate to face in a different direction. "That's Dee Dee, Trey's wife."

Kate indulged in a look to appease the woman's gossipy nature. The object of Estelle's interest was a glossy blonde, her hair white gold, her face as smooth and classically structured as a princess's. She stood next to the shrimp lover.

"You'd have a great deal in common."

Kate doubted *that*.

"They're such darling people. They invited Lisa to spend time with them in Newport before the America's Cup." Estelle's hand fluttered to her pearl choker. "I really am at a loss as to whether or not to let her go. I'll have to think more about that. But you should meet Dee Dee. She lives for music."

Kate finally understood what Estelle was getting at.

"She's chairperson for the young people's concert. I'll introduce you two." She scanned the room as if she were at a tennis match. "I wonder where Kippy is. Oh, well, I'll find the dear boy later. But—I did want to talk to you alone about something else."

Annoyingly, Kate felt Estelle's arm hook with hers as she stole a glance in Brian's direction.

"We must start introducing you to some suitable men."

Kate doubted that she veiled her surprise or her annoyance at the woman's comment. Only Brian's sudden appearance at her side kept both emotions from erupting.

Estelle offered him a strained smile. "I must mingle now. I'll introduce you later to some friends, Katherine."

Brian handed her a plate.

"Did you hear her?"

"Don't worry about it, Kate. I learned years ago that sometimes even blood-of-their-blood doesn't measure up."

"Have you been busy?" she asked before biting into a shrimp.

"Stimulated."

She dabbed a finger at the corner of her mouth. "By what?"

"Not what I want to be stimulated by. Discussions about articles in the *Harvard Law Review* and the *Wall Street Journal*."

"You aren't comfortable, are you?"

"Feeling out of synch with my surroundings. I always did. I always though that they take themselves too seriously. And they always had upper-class misgivings about me. They'd hide the silverware."

"You do go on, Fleming. I know you. I'm sure you had a great deal of fun leading them on."

"Nudge me if I get started again." With his fork, he pushed a green pepper out of the salad and to the edge of his plate. "What was Estelle bending your ear about?"

Kate snatched up the green pepper from his plate. "Her daughter. The poor child has a sensitive stomach, according to her mother. But Lisa is far from frail," Kate assured him. "She puts away a dozen cookies after her lesson." She sighed as she noticed Estelle beckoning her to cross the room to join her. "What is it with her?"

Brian grinned. "Find out what she wants, then we'll dance."

"A reward." Dimples cut into her cheeks. "I'll hurry back." But not fast enough, Brian thought as he inched his way toward the white-coated servant behind a bar. If he had one more glass of champagne, he'd retch.

Several minutes later, a glass of Scotch in his hand, he retraced his path to where he'd left Kate. Brian froze at the sight of her sandwiched between Estelle and another woman.

Kate listened to Estelle expounding about the other woman's contributions to promoting funding for the symphony. She stole a glance toward Brian, wondering if she could signal to him to rescue her.

His eyes made contact with hers for only a second. As he began weaving his way around clusters of people and heading toward the exit, her apprehension got the best of her. She cut into Estelle's monologue and excused herself.

She stared at the stiff straightness of Brian's back and sensed more than his purposeful stride was putting distance between them. "Where are you going?" she asked as she caught up with him in the foyer.

"I have to leave."

"Leave?" she asked louder than she'd intended. "Why? Why are you leaving?"

"I don't want to stay."

"Then I'm going, too."

"Don't be stupid."

"We came together. We leave together," Kate insisted.

A strange, unfathomable tenseness strained his features. "You can't go," he said on a sigh.

"If you are, I am."

She saw indecision in his face. His gaze cut from her to the butler holding his coat and then back to her. Brian shook his head at the tall, stately man. "I won't be leaving yet."

With a turn of his shoulder, he made her feel as if they were strangers. "We only have to stay a little longer," she said.

He leaned back against the doorway. His jaw tense, he seemed engaged in a private battle.

"I know you're not happy to be here, but why are you suddenly so...?"

"I've no excuse. I'm sorry."

His apology came across as cold and unfeeling.

"There you are," came a grating nasal voice.

Brian met the man with a challenging look. "Kate, this is Mitch Van Hammon."

Kate grasped what was happening.

"My ex-brother-in-law," Brian added, sounding less pugnacious.

Mitch Van Hammon looked her over. "I'd hoped you'd introduce me to your—your companion."

Kate produced a smile, but had to grit her teeth at the man's baiting attitude.

He looked away as if distracted. "I must find Arden. Her family has a Mercedes dealership now, and I'm eager for a new car."

"Why? Are you driving a year-old Porsche?" Brian quipped.

Their gazes clashed.

"I'd forgotten your droll sense of humor, Fleming."

Kate held her silence until Brian had no choice but to stop tossing visual daggers at the man's back and face her. "Now will you tell me what is going on?"

"Would you dance with me?"

"Will you talk to me?"

He lifted her hand and kissed her palm. "Yes, but I need to hold you."

More confused than ever she followed him onto the dance floor.

Shadows emphasized the hard angles and the hollows in his face. "Estelle's been a bosom buddy tonight."

"I'm one of the right kind suddenly," Kate said. "She told me all kinds of little secrets."

"What kinds of little secrets?"

At his sudden crushing grip, she frowned at their joined hands. His touch changed to a gentler one, but his expression was unfamiliarly fierce. "I told you already about Lisa's fragile stomach." Kate pressed her cheek against his. "Some friends of Estelle's, the blond Ken and Barbie, invited Lisa to spend time on their yacht."

"I saw you talking to the blonde."

"Barbie?"

"That's not her name."

"Dee Dee. She has connections with the symphony." At his silence, she looked up at him. "I was telling her that I was looking for musicians..." She paused, responding to his frown with one of her own. "For the banquet? Remember the banquet?"

"What's wrong with Burly Mead?"

Needing to remind herself and him of a shared intimacy, she ran her fingers in a caress over the hair at the nape of his neck. "Nothing. But the woman knows a great many musicians and could—"

"I don't want her help."

Her body tensed in his arms. "All right." Annoyance slipped into her voice. "I realize seeing your ex-brother-in-law wasn't pleasant. But for the record, you're acting like a pain in the neck."

"No," he returned in a low hard whisper. "Seeing my ex-wife put me in this mood. Seeing my ex-wife having a chummy conversation with you put me in this mood."

"Dee Dee?"

He shrugged. "She's got a new husband and took a new nickname."

Her throat was dry. "I didn't know."

"I should have expected we'd see them here. You're probably going to run into them often. You're part of—"

"I'm not any different," she returned. But suddenly her life was very complicated. Tread carefully, she warned herself. They both were teetering on the edge of their emotions. The concern on his face tugged at her heart. She pressed her hand tighter against the back of his neck. "You're a very good dancer."

He forced a grin. "I'm especially good at whirling around the dance floor toward the exit."

A smile tugged at her lips. "Right out the door?"

"Right out the door."

"I couldn't do that."

"What could you do?"

"Say good-night and depart politely."

"Politely, huh?"

Her eyes sparkled. "And quickly."

"And then?"

"Then, we'll see what the night brings."

Brian awoke with a start, annoyed as a dream of midnight and Kate was snatched from him. A hint of rose streaked across the gray sky. He fought to orient himself and glanced at the clock. Five-thirty. Morning? Night? Morning, he decided, and finally registered what had jarred him from his sleep. The phone shrilled several more times before he reached out blindly for the receiver. He fumbled and dislodged it from the cradle. On the carpet a distant male voice drifted out of the receiver and up at him. "Hello? Hello?"

He grabbed the cord. The voice continued to bellow from the dangling receiver. Holding the mouthpiece close, he demanded, "Who is this?"

"Tom."

Kate shifted beside him and uttered a soft moan. "Who?"

"An insane man." Brian looked down at her and lifted his arm to release her hair that had been trapped beneath it. "It's five-thirty, Tom. Five-thirty in the morning."

"Is it? Woke you?"

"Damn, I hate it when you're on the graveyard shift."

"As long as you're awake."

"I'm not."

"You're talking."

Brian closed his eyes as Kate turned into him. Warm and naked, she was inviting. "What do you want?" he asked Tom between nibbles at her ear.

"I called to tell you the music was great."

"Music?"

"Burly Mead. The committee gave him a unanimous nod of approval. We've got everything set up for the banquet, but I need you to do something else for me."

Kate stretched beside him, pushing her length against him and draping a leg over his.

Brian groaned. "What do you want, Tom?"

"You're surly in the morning, aren't you?"

"Talk."

"I contacted a party shop that's about four blocks from your house. Could you pick up the crates of decorations Friday? I'll meet you at the banquet hall that evening to help put them up."

"Yeah," Brian said, wiling to agree to anything to end the phone conversation.

"And see if you can get your sister to help."

He felt the steady thump of Kate's heart. Her skin felt hot, enticingly hot.

"And Kate," Tom added.

Yes, and Kate. Brian shifted to push himself against her. She was a part of his life now. He wanted her in it forever. But would she choose to be, choose him? "Goodbye, Tom," he said distractedly before dropping the phone back onto the floor.

He heard the soft click that ended the connection, and with lazy pleasure, he ran a hand down Kate's hip and then back up again. She responded to his touch as if it were as natural as breathing. Doubts fled. She'd choose him. His life. His love. "You make me weak," he murmured.

She moaned a little. It was sufficient encouragement. He scooted down, fanning his fingers across her buttocks, pressing warm, light kisses down her breast. He felt her hands in his hair as he circled her breast with his tongue. Pleasure came on a rush as if he'd never known her softness before, as if her body wasn't familiar to him. Each time with her was a little different, a little more bonding.

She whispered his name, her hands suddenly coursing over him, her heart hammering harder beneath his lips. Reason abandoned him. He touched the softness of her belly, the firmness of her thigh. He sought with his hands and then with his mouth the places that gave him pleasure, then caressed those that gave her pleasure.

When he thought his need to love her would hurl him to the brink of insanity, he buried his face in her neck and entered her. He drove deeply until his breaths were ragged, torn from his throat, until nothing would satisfy him except filling her, meeting his passion, seeking the peak of hers.

For long moments after, he stared at the sunlight streaming into the room and listened to her breathing, steadier now. His own still filled the room with raspy sighs. He felt fatigued. Wonderfully exhausted. He hadn't lied. She made him weak. Yet, she made him strong. She made him feel indestructible.

As she cuddled closer, he pressed his lips to her cheek. "How about a movie tonight?"

"Tonight's okay."

"Busy today?"

Her breath fanned his chest. "A morning with Breshkov and a student. Lunch with Gertrude." She yawned. "Afternoon—" she yawned again "—new student."

"Big day." He caressed her hair, smoothing it down, marveling at the softness being as silky as he once had imagined.

"What?" she asked sleepily.

"Will he tell you whether he's accepted you or not?"

"I have to play once more for him. Today," she murmured.

At her sleepy incoherence, he kissed her forehead. "Good luck, sweetheart."

"Hmm."

Tenderness, love, fear mingled within him. Sharp, conflicting emotions. So many things were happening in her life, he realized. He tugged her tighter to him. There had to be room for him.

Though Kate left Brian early enough to be on time for her audition, she made a mistake and stopped at her apartment. First Gertrude called, then Estelle. Politely, Kate listened while she repeatedly glanced at the clock.

Somehow she reached the music academy on time, but her stomach was tied in knots while she played.

As she finished the final crescendo, then lightened her touch for the softer decreasing whispery notes, she felt displeasure. She sat exhausted before the keyboard and saw Breshkov's scowl. She could have done better, played with more spirit, more feeling.

"Thank you, Miss Lindstrom." His voice was curt, commanding her to vacate the piano bench.

Kate stood mechanically. She swallowed against a constricting tightness in her throat, turned and then grabbed her coat from a nearby chair. "Thank you for the opportunity to play for you again."

He gave her a quick, dismissing nod.

She stepped outside, feeling too numb to notice the bitter wind. The warmth from the studio fanned her back as the door closed behind her. She felt more than the simple physical barrier of a man-made door. She should have practiced more. She should have spent time the night before doing rapid scale runs.

Instead she'd stood at a party among strangers, trying to feel as if she'd belonged there. She'd nodded and responded at all the right moments to Gertrude and Estelle and the infamous Dee Dee. Yet, beneath those well-timed smiles and proper comments, she'd never lost the sense of playacting.

For a long moment Kate sat in her car, her hands clenched in her lap. She'd wanted a position with Breshkov more than anything. She'd wanted to please him.

Draping her arms across the steering wheel and leaning forward, she rested her forehead against her arms. Why had she forgotten that and allowed herself to be distracted? she wondered as she gave into disappointment. What had happened? Where was the music in her life?

During the next two hours her mood didn't improve. She returned to her apartment as Billy Newman arrived for his lesson. It didn't go well.

Impatient, Kate watched him grimace as he hit another wrong note. "You didn't practice again, did you?" she questioned.

He turned his face up to her, his soft brown eyes appealing to her not to scold.

Kate glanced at the clock, aware she'd have to rush to meet Gertrude for lunch. "Billy, the lesson is over for today," she said curtly. "Go home. Practice. If you don't and aren't more prepared when you come for your next lesson, I'm going to talk to your parents."

Head down, he slid off the piano bench.

Kate handed him his jacket.

"No cookies?" he asked.

The young face staring up at her looked dejected. Even when he'd done poorly before, she'd never skipped the cookie time. Usually she insisted on it after a bad lesson. Kate shook her head. "Not today." She glanced at the clock again.

He turned away, heading for the door.

Kate felt a knot forming in her stomach. "Do you want to take some with you?"

He looked back with sad brown eyes. "No, thank you."

Kate released a long, hard breath as the door closed behind him. Why was everything suddenly going wrong?

She charged toward the bedroom to change clothes. She couldn't seem to please anyone anymore, she reflected, yanking a simple ivory-colored dress from a hanger. Not anyone. She eyed the dress and tossed it on the bed. Not even herself, she decided, reaching for a navy suit.

* * *

Brian noted her quietness, her forced smiles that evening. He fought his own insecurities and said nothing. But if someone had asked him about the movie, he doubted if he could have recalled one scene from it.

Though uneasy, he waited until they were inching their way with the crowd exiting the theater to guess at Kate's problem. "How did the lunch date go?"

"Okay."

"Just okay." Brian linked his hand with hers.

She stared out at the parking lot. "Where did you park your car?"

"In the Apples section."

Kate smiled. "I never remember where I park. It was a good movie, wasn't it?"

"Uh-huh. Tell me what happened with Breshkov."

Kate leaned back against the car door. "I didn't play well."

"But he didn't tell you that he wasn't still considering you, did he?"

She lifted her face and stared up at the sky. "I don't know if he is. I'm not sure."

"Modesty?"

"Honesty. I've played better."

He opened the car door for her. "You've had a lot on your mind."

As she slid into the car, she added, "I'm not sure that I want a position with him anymore."

Brian took his time rounding the car and sliding in behind the steering wheel. He flicked on the ignition. The car hummed, cutting into the silence between them. "Why did you say that?"

"Gertrude and Douglas asked me to go to Palm Springs with them in a few weeks."

"What about Breshkov?"

She turned her face away.

Brian shifted the car into drive and pulled out of the parking space. "If he accepts you, wouldn't you be working with him by then?"

"Yes, but I told you. I'm not sure that I will be."

"I thought it was what you wanted."

"I want to please them," Kate snapped.

He was silent, feeling as if he'd somehow stepped on a merry-go-round that he'd sworn three years ago never to ride again.

Kate resisted an urge to squirm. She could hear his unspoken questions. Though he'd said nothing, before the evening ended, she knew that he'd insist on answers to what was bothering him.

When he parked the car at the curb in front of her building, he reacted predictably. "Are they aware that you were trying to get a position with Breshkov?"

Kate pushed open the car door. "That doesn't really suit them."

"It doesn't really..." He drew a long breath. "I thought they cared about you."

"They do!" She slammed the car door and hurried up the steps.

He met her at the apartment building door. "Seems to me they aren't worrying too much about what you want. Only what they want."

"They have a certain image to present." Kate unlocked the door quickly.

"And being one of them, so do you?"

"Yes."

His fingers closed tightly around her hand as they ascended the steps. "Kate," he said softly, nearly undoing her.

She waited until she reached her apartment door, then struggled to meet his searching eyes. "They want me to open my own studio."

"Is that what you want?"

She bent her head to unlock the apartment door. Though dark within, she could see the outline of her spinet. How simple life had been weeks ago, she thought. How wonderfully simple. "I think so," she finally answered.

Chapter Thirteen

During the next week Kate juggled her time. A hectic schedule left her feeling frazzled, her life suddenly split into time segments for students, for the Strantons and for Brian.

As Lisa Manington finished her lesson, the buzzer announced Estelle's arrival. Forty-five minutes later, Estelle, more long-winded and chummy than usual, still rambled on about her dinner party Saturday night for Trey and Dee Dee.

"You know she was married before," Estelle informed her.

Here it comes, Kate told herself. "Yes."

"I knew it wouldn't last. He's not our kind. Gertrude has spoken to you about meeting Buffy Smithson, hasn't she?"

"I've met him," Kate responded.

"You have! What did you think of him?"

Buffy with the big ears, the Rolls and the roving hands. "Different," Kate answered. "I'm really sorry to rush you, Estelle, but I have an appointment."

The other woman's mouth snapped shut.

Determined to be firm, Kate squared her shoulders and led Lisa toward the door.

Accepting the cue, Estelle joined them. "An appointment with Verdelli?"

"Who?"

"Everyone goes to him." She eyed Kate's hair. "You should, too. Not that your hair isn't lovely, but his salon works miracles."

Kate attempted a semblance of a smile while resisting a temptation to match the woman's rudeness. "I must hurry."

Estelle nodded and followed her daughter out the door. Somehow Kate managed not to slam it.

Perched on the edge of the desk in the records office at city hall, Brian impatiently tapped a pencil against the wood edge. Without preamble, he rushed his words when his sister finally answered the phone. "Brie, is Kate there?"

"Hold the line. I've got another call."

Brian continued the rhythmic beat with his pencil. The woman behind the desk glared. "Sorry." He gave her a smile and set down the pencil.

"She's not here," Sabrina announced.

"She said that she'd help."

"She probably got busy. I know the feeling," she grumbled. "The office phone has been ringing off the hook. Are you coming in soon?"

"I have to pick up those decorations first. Put on the answering machine."

"Hey, don't yell at me."

"Don't yell at me, then."

"Brian, take it easy. She'll get here."

He released a long breath, not liking his edginess any more than she did. "I'm sorry."

"Me, too. Do you need a sister's shoulder?"

He forced a bright note into his voice for her sake. "They're not very broad."

"Broad enough."

"Thanks, anyway." He set the receiver back in its cradle, damning himself for taking out his uncertainty about Kate on Sabrina. But lately, instead of feeling closer to Kate, he sensed an invisible wall being erected between them. A wall that the Strantons had started. And he couldn't shake the feeling that he was losing her.

Nothing about her days was normal lately, Kate mused as she rushed up the steps to Brian's office. So much had happened so fast. All her life she'd known emptiness. He wanted to fill it. Though he hadn't said he loved her, she sensed it every time he looked at her, every time he touched her. But other people wanted to fill that emptiness in her life, too. She found their demands nerve-racking. Life used to be simple, she reflected again, almost aching for the sereneness, the peace of mind, the self-satisfaction she'd known before.

"Am I late?" she questioned as she pushed open the office door. Seeing Sabrina setting down the receiver, she grimaced, "Sorry. I didn't know you were on the phone."

"You missed his call by a second. What a pain."

Kate grinned at her.

"He's not an easy man.

One of many in her life, Kate reflected while yanking off her gloves and thinking about Breshkov. She hadn't heard from him since her second audition.

"I guess my brother's worth the effort," Sabrina added in a teasing voice.

"I know that."

Sabrina leaned back in her chair. "When he was hurt before, I thought then that he'd never pull out of it."

"Are you talking about his marriage to De—Diane?"

Sabrina swiveled her chair away from the desk. "She was so sweet on him in the beginning. For a sharp guy, he was blind to her faults."

"She is beautiful."

"You've met her?"

Kate nodded and settled on the closest chair. "He doesn't talk about her very much."

"Not to anyone."

"I know her parents interfered."

"She didn't do anything about preventing that." Sabrina's eyes sparkled. "I'm really happy that he met you." She grinned. "I never could get close to Diane, and I always did want a sister."

Kate froze as Sabrina's words registered. She was talking about a commitment that Kate hadn't even considered.

Brian stood in the doorway, his left arm numb from the weight of the carton he held. As Kate flashed a smile at him, he suddenly didn't feel any pain. He didn't feel the worry that had nagged at him for days. Nothing had changed between them, he told himself.

"So, you've finally arrived," Sabrina quipped.

"Ladies," he announced, ignoring his sister's irritated tone, "have I got a deal for you."

"Here it comes," Sabrina said out of the corner of her mouth in a stage whisper.

Kate participated in the tease. "The sell job?"

"He wants help."

"Would you stop a tradition?" He turned his most guilt-provoking look first on one and then the other.

"What tradition?" Kate asked hesitantly.

"Think back to *Tom Sawyer*."

Sabrina slammed a desk drawer. "I refuse to paint a fence."

"I refuse to let you," he shot back.

Though she looked insulted, she winked. "What's wrong with my painting?"

"You helped me paint a bedroom. Do you remember that?"

"I did a good job."

He rolled his eyes at Kate. "She painted herself." He slid the carton onto a nearby table. "And all I need today is a sharp female with a decorator's eye." He gave Kate a meaningful look.

"He obviously means you," Sabrina said after the fact.

"And for your help, I'll give a reward."

As he knelt down before her on one knee, Kate suppressed laughter.

"Popcorn," he announced brightly, whipping an enormous bag out from behind his back.

"All for me?"

"Whether you help or not, you get the reward."

She responded to his lopsided grin and bent forward to place her hands on his shoulders. "Not what I had in mind," she whispered.

"I like the way you think." He kissed her quickly, then stood. "Who said women only like flowers?" he asked his sister.

Sabrina leaned back on her chair. "Don't romantic men send your heart pitter-pattering?"

"Have you ever read his limericks?" Kate asked in a conspiratorial tone.

"Hey, hey, leave my poetry alone." While Kate tugged on her gloves, Brian tossed his sister's boots toward her. "Get up."

"I didn't plan on going with you. I have so much to—"

"Come on. We need help."

"Brian . . ." She started to protest.

He flicked on the answering machine.

"We'll probably miss the greatest case of our lives," she mumbled, but reached for her coat.

"I'll chance it. Come on," he urged while picking up the carton. "Hurry up."

Meeting him at the door, Kate sent him a questioning look.

Tom, Brian mouthed.

She leaned forward and whispered, "You are a romantic soul."

He kissed her, only their lips touching. "Damn box," he grumbled.

"Enough of that." Sabrina passed between them and out the door. "I'd better not be the only one helping there," she insisted. "Or you're going to owe me more than a bag of popcorn."

* * *

"I didn't know he'd be here." Sabrina glared across the room at Tom.

Kate stood on a ladder and inserted a tack through a streamer. "I gather you don't like him."

Sabrina gave her a quick but forced smile. "It's not important." She held the other end of the streamer while Kate twisted it. "They'll have flowers delivered tomorrow afternoon."

"It looks nice."

"It always does. Even the first year, when they had this banquet in a VFW hall, I thought it was beautiful."

Kate paused and looked down at her. "Because it's in your dad's honor?"

Sabrina nodded. "Sometimes I have to charge myself up before presenting the award. I'm a real sob sister," she admitted in a humorous tone.

"You both are very proud of your father, aren't you?"

"He was the best."

Kate pushed her thumb against the tack. Despite the welcome that she'd received from the Strantons, she doubted if she'd ever experience the feeling for either of them that Sabrina and Brian had felt for their father.

"Your pop was a special breed," someone commented in passing to Brian.

Brian continued to put chairs around tables.

"Sure miss your old man," a crew-cut bull of a man said.

Me, too, Brian reflected. He grabbed two more chairs from a stack against the wall.

A soft-looking, middle-aged redhead grinned at him. "You look just like him. You know, I never noticed that before, Brian." She sighed. "He was a wonderful fella. Did you know I had my eye on him?"

Brian sent her a teasing grin. "When was that?"

"Before he married your mother." She touched his arm. "And after. But his heart belonged to one woman."

Brian knew the feeling. *I'm just like you, Dad,* he thought. *I don't regret that, but I sure wish that you'd stuck around long enough to tell me how to win her.*

"You're getting as bad as Uncle Charley," Tom gibed as he reached for another stack of chairs. "Every few minutes he stops to daydream and leaves the work for the rest of us."

"You really look overworked."

Tom shot a glance at Sabrina. "Only when I attempt a conversation with your sister."

"Sweet and congenial as usual, is she?"

"To me."

"She needs to fall in love again."

"Yeah, she does." Tom inclined his head. "Why the frown? Your life is going great right now, isn't it?"

"Everybody has some problems."

"So what's the problem between you and Kate?"

Brian grinned. "Always second-guessing, detective?"

"Guessed right, didn't I?"

Brian nodded. "The Strantons asked her to consider opening a studio of her own."

"Can she afford that?"

"They probably offered money for it."

"Are you feeling unable to compete?"

Brian frowned. "No." He shrugged. "Although at one time, that would have bothered me."

"You're losing me. What's happening? She wants to accept their offer and you don't want her to? She doesn't want to accept their offer? What?"

"I don't know."

"You're in love with the woman, and you don't know?"

"It's been a confusing time lately."

"Doesn't she teach in her home?" At Brian's nod, Tom asked, "Then why is she opening the studio? If she doesn't want it, then—"

"Pressure. The Strantons believe people will get the wrong impression about her association with them if she doesn't have her own studio."

"Piano teacher in second-floor apartment—"

"Third."

"—third-floor apartment doesn't have the right image?"

"Something like that."

"Is that the problem between you two?"

"No," Brian responded.

"Hey, who's got the problem? You or her?"

Brian looked away. Tom was treading too close. "You," he countered in a lighter tone, and glanced at his sister.

"Yeah, me," Tom agreed with a look at Sabrina. "Who can understand women," he added before he carted away more chairs.

Brian stared across the room. He saw no one except Kate. Standing on a ladder, she offered him a view that he never tired of. With a simple stretching motion, she stirred his blood.

"Okay, brother dear," Sabrina quipped.

He jumped at the sound of her voice. "What?" he asked, practically growling the question.

"When did you become so jittery?"

"When did you become so quiet?"

Sabrina made a face at him. "Kate could use some help."

"I thought you were helping her."

"Don't refuse a gift."

"Never." He laughed and affectionately shoved her with his elbow in passing. Kate had made him love again. And remember. And feel afraid. But of what? Who she could be? He already knew who she was. A woman with so much forgiveness in her that if the Strantons had offered her nothing but love, she'd have been satisfied.

Brian stopped beside the ladder and touched her hip. "I'm your new helper."

"All help is appreciated."

"Do you realize that you didn't even look to see who put his hand on you?"

"Who would dare but you?"

"Are you almost done?"

She looked over her shoulder at him.

"I know a great place that serves pistachio ice-cream cones."

As she took a step down, he wrapped his arm around her. Slowly he brought her feet to the ground.

"You could turn a woman's head that way."

His arms remained loosely around her back. "With pistachio ice-cream cones?"

"No. Other things."

"Want to forget the ice cream?"

"I never gave it a thought."

* * *

Kate finished dressing at six-thirty Saturday night. For nearly a half hour she'd debated about which dress to wear. Her inability to make any decision lately was driving her crazy. But she'd felt so much pressure, so many demands. The Strantons wanted her to be one of them, while Brian urged her to join him in a simple duet. No wonder she felt as if she was losing control of her life. She'd always been a soloist, aware she could get hurt if she gave too much of herself. How could she explain that fear, make the Strantons—and Brian—understand that? How could she when she didn't even understand what was wrong? She finally had everything she'd ever wanted. She should be blissful. So why wasn't she?

For several seconds she pushed her hair up, then let it drop back to her shoulders. Disgusted, she shoved the strands back up and pushed pins into them and prayed that she didn't have to make one more decision before the night was over.

As if an omen of things to come, the phone rang. She wavered about answering it, but considered that Brian might have had car trouble, any kind of trouble. She wanted to be there for him as he'd been there for her.

On a sigh, she picked up the receiver. "Hello."

"Katherine, it's Aunt Gertrude."

Kate instantly tensed.

"Did you know that a party was being given for Trey and Dee Dee Dossin this evening?"

"Estelle mentioned it."

"It would be lovely if you could come."

"I—I can't—"

"It would please me if you'd try."

"I—" The refusal lodged in her throat. *Say it, dammit,* she demanded of herself. *Tell her that you can't.*

"Katherine."

Kate flinched at the buzz of the doorbell. "Someone is—Brian is here. I promised him that I'd—"

"Katherine, you have certain responsibilities now."

She stretched the telephone cord to push the button that opened the downstairs door. "What responsibilities?"

"My dear, you're a Stranton."

Brian knocked, then pushed open Kate's apartment door. Her profile to him, she stared at the telephone on the table before her. She looked stunning, her back straight, her chin high, her hands resting in the lap of a soft blue dress. As he stepped in, she turned her head.

She blinked several times as if she had been caught up in some trance. "I'm ready."

"You look beautiful."

Her lips curved in a smile, but he noted the tremble. Stepping closer, he was tempted to stop, frame her face in his hands and kiss her long and hard. Instead, he circled to take her coat from her. Briefly his fingertips grazed hers in the exchange. He felt the tension—hers and his own. He fought old doubts. "Is something wrong?"

"Gertrude just called."

"And?"

Her eyes met his. "She wants me to go to Estelle's party tonight."

He waited, needing time to measure his reply. "It'll be late when the banquet is over. Did she want you to come after?"

"Instead of."

"And what do you want?" he asked, tense.

"To please them."

"What about me?"

A frown formed a line between her eyebrows. He saw her indecisiveness. He sensed her confusion. But his anger and his hurt took command. "What about me?" he insisted. "I love you. Does that count?"

She stared silently back at him.

He felt young and awkward and vulnerable for the first time in years. "This isn't the reaction I was hoping for." As she shook her head and took a step back, an ache swelled up within him. He wanted to bridge the distance between them, grab her, pull her close. He wanted time to back up. Just for a few seconds, he thought. Back up and let everything be different.

"Why now?" she asked, her voice shaking.

"What?"

"Why did you say that tonight?"

"What difference does it make when I say it? All that matters is what you say back."

She didn't move or say a word.

"Kate?"

"I—I... Please don't be hurt. I just don't know—"

"You don't know what? If you love me or if you'll ever love me? What! What don't you know?"

"I don't even know who I am anymore," she yelled back at him. "I can't explain. Trust. Love. Why now? I've never known them before. Why should so many people want to give them to me now?"

"I don't care about them. I only know what I feel. I love you. I want to marry you. I want to spend the rest of my life with you."

She squeezed her eyes shut for a second.

"Tell me." His hands gripped her arms, insisting on her attention, forcing her to look at him. "Tell me what you want."

"I don't know what I want anymore."

He heard her voice crack. He knew she was close to tears, and still he pushed. "Do you want me?"

"Brian..." She pulled back. "Yes, but..." She shook her head. "No one was ever there for me before. No one."

"Haven't I been?"

"Yes, you have. And you scare me," she whispered.

He saw tears in her eyes and took a step forward to hold her. As she backed up, he stopped and raised his hands, his palms up. "I don't understand."

"I'm afraid I'll get used to you being there for me, and you won't be." She took another step back. "I can handle being alone again. I've done that all my life. But I couldn't stand the feeling of not being wanted by you once I'd known it."

"That won't happen."

"You can't make that promise."

"So you've made your choice."

She shook her head. "I've made no choices."

"Yes, you have. I told you I love you. And you can't say the words back. I tell you that I want to marry you, and you don't say yes."

"Brian—try to understand."

"You've made a choice, Kate. It's clear to me."

"You still don't understand. Suddenly everyone says they want a part of me. They want to be part of my life."

He drew a hard breath. "Not me," he said in a firm voice.

She stared in a dazed stupor at him, tears bright in her eyes.

He fought the anger and the tenderness for her that made him want to accept anything she'd offer. "I don't want you just for this moment. I want you forever. And I don't want a part of you. I want all of your love. If I can't have that, I don't want to be a part of any of your life."

"Brian," she called out as he headed toward the door.

He stopped. He had to fight himself. So easily he could turn, he could pull her into his arms, he could be hurt again.

"Brian, it wasn't supposed to end like this."

Not turning around, he curled a hand around the doorknob. "It wasn't supposed to end."

Chapter Fourteen

Kate wanted to cry, to release the anguish inside her. She hadn't meant to hurt him. He was the last person she wanted to hurt. But fear sparked different responses in different people. She was feeling suffocated, swallowed up by too many people all claiming they cared about her. Did anyone?

She slipped off her shoes and leaned back against a sofa cushion. With a sigh, she stared down at her dress. *All dressed up and no place to go,* she thought. *Feel sorry for yourself. Feel sorry because you're suddenly being offered more than you'd ever expected and you're scared stiff to accept any of it.* She grimaced. Life was so full of irony. Here she was, scared to death of the love she'd always yearned for.

* * *

Sabrina breezed across the room, her peach chiffon skirt swishing with her movements. "I thought you were going to be late."

Brian scanned the room crowded with couples. "Every table is filled, huh?"

Sabrina placed a hand on his chest. "Yes." She looked around. "Where's Kate?"

"At home. How long before dinner is served?"

"What do you mean, 'at home'"

"At home, Brie," he answered in a controlled tone. "It's over."

Her head tilted slightly.

"She has what she wants."

"And you?"

He slid an arm around her shoulder and turned her to walk with him. "Come on. I can use a little sisterly sympathy tonight."

Kate stared out the window. Why hadn't she told him that she loved him? Afraid. Always afraid, she reflected. How could she ever explain the rejection she'd always felt and was shielding herself from feeling again?

"Katie." A soft rap on the door followed the sound of Liz's voice.

Kate squared her shoulders. "Come in, Liz."

A coat in her hand, Liz offered a Cheshire-cat grin. "Hi. And goodbye."

Kate pushed herself off the sofa. "Goodbye. Where are you going?"

"With Harry."

Kate rushed to her. "With—"

"Be happy for me."

Kate hugged her. "I am." She laughed. "And surprised. Do you have time to tell me what happened?"

Liz pulled back and slowly nodded. "Yes, I have a few minutes. We're going on a trip. A second honeymoon. Do you believe that?"

"How—what convinced you?"

"He did. He told me that he'd begun to feel as if I'd forgotten that he existed. I didn't think that was true. He was the one who was always at work. But do you know what he said? He said he was working for me—to give me everything I ever wanted."

"There wasn't another woman?"

"No." Liz ran a hand across the back of her cropped hair. "We both acted dumb. All either of us wanted was each other. When he said that he wanted more space, the lovable but uncommunicative idiot meant that he was tired, that he needed to relax more. I wouldn't give him a chance to explain. I believed that he wanted to be footloose. That was my fault."

Kate struggled not to reveal her own mood but a weariness weakened her. "Do you believe him?"

Liz's smile slipped. "Believe him? Yes. I love him."

"He could hurt you again."

Puzzled, Liz blinked rapidly. "Yes, he could. But that's the risk of loving, isn't it?" She swept a look down Kate's dress. "Where were you going tonight?"

"A banquet."

"With Brian?"

Kate turned away and, balancing herself, she slipped on one shoe and then the other. "Yes."

"Oh, I won't keep you then. I just wanted to share my news."

Kate reached for her coat. "I'm not headed there." She hugged Liz again. "I'm really happy for you."

"I'm happy for me, too," she announced as Kate urged her toward the door. "But I'd liked to know the reason for your long face."

"Is that what you see?"

"Down to the floor."

Kate managed a token laugh. "Where are you and Harry going?"

Her hand touched Kate's arm. "Katie?"

Kate shook her head.

Liz sighed heavily. "Hawaii. We're going to Hawaii. First." She grinned, stepping into the hall ahead of Kate. "Then, who knows where? You know, it's funny, I thought that he wanted this super career woman. Someone with her own business. So I struggled to be what he wanted. But that wasn't what I wanted. My biological clock is ticking. I want kids. I won't give up my business, but instead of planning parties for other people's kids, I want to plan some for my own."

"Did you tell him that?"

"Finally. Idiots." Liz sighed. "We've been idiots. He thought I wanted a jet-set life-style and a mansion somewhere, so he worked like a fool to give me that. We were working hard to meet each other's wants, but we weren't getting closer. We were pushing each other away."

Kate curled a hand around the banister as they descended the steps.

"Where are you going now? To Brian?"

Kate shook her head. "The Strantons."

Tom clamped a hand on Brian's shoulder. "Are you holding up the bar tonight?"

"This is only my second."

"Your sister finally talked to me."

Brian arched an eyebrow.

"To ask me to come over here and talk to you."

Brian stared into his drink. "There's nothing to talk about. Not anymore."

Tom's fingers cut into Brian's shoulder. "Come on," he urged. "We should sit for dinner."

Brian followed him to the table, but he doubted that he'd hear the speeches or taste the food.

Kate stood outside the Strantons' home. The air bit at her flesh, and snow brushed her skin, but she felt the warmth of satisfaction spreading through her. She drew long breaths as she walked toward her car. Recently, she'd felt suffocated. She hadn't been comfortable with the Strantons' insistence to do this and do that. She'd resisted Brian's demand for an answer. Did she love him? Of course, she loved him. But that question had been one more on a list of too many for her.

She'd wanted to belong, to be loved. She'd yearned for those feelings for so long that she'd been willing to do anything to please other people and to win their love. But like Harry and Liz had learned, she couldn't be somebody else just to make others happy. She'd been so worried about pleasing others, she'd forgotten about herself. Whether her name was Lindstrom or Stranton, she had to please herself first.

Brian pushed his fork around the dessert plate. Some crazy notion had made him believe and hope that Kate would suddenly appear.

He was a fool. He'd sat through dinner, and now dessert, playing a mental game with himself. It wasn't the first one he'd played. He'd done the same with Diane, believing one thing when the exact opposite was true.

Speeches now, he noted as someone stepped to the microphone. The presentation of the award. Then music. And then he could leave.

Sorry, Dad, I just can't hang in here this year. But you're missed more than ever. A hell of a lot, Brian realized. Despite the years since his father's death, Brian still missed him. But good memories mingled now with the misery of his death—days of fishing in a boat, lunches on a park bench during breaks in an investigation, evenings at home watching a basketball game.

Brian heard laughter and glanced around at the smiling faces. Their camaraderie, their happiness flowed through the room as if timed to force him to remember all the laughter he'd known as a child, all the people who'd cared about his father. Didn't Kate deserve the same? He knew how important family was. He doubted he could make a choice that would eliminate his family from his life. And he had no right to ask her to do that. If he wanted her, he had to push aside doubts about the Strantons' wealth.

Push, he mused. The magic word. He had pushed her too hard. He'd added to her confusion by demanding that she make a choice. His pride had demanded it.

He needed to push himself now. Push aside his pride and face the truth about what had really caused the end of his marriage to Diane. He had to stop running from it and admit that wealth hadn't been the problem between him and his ex-wife.

Brian settled back on his chair. As the emcee returned to the microphone, Brian gently nudged his sister. "That's your cue."

"Why don't you present the award this year?"

"Your face is prettier."

"Don't go soft on me," she whispered. "I'll think some alien inhabited your body."

He produced a smile because he knew she wanted to see it.

"Here goes." As she pushed back her chair, Tom half stood.

Sabrina glared; Tom shrugged. He appeared caught between embarrassment and resignation about his obvious feelings for her.

"Hang in there," Brian said low to Tom before joining in the applause at the emcee's announcement of the Thomas Fleming Award. Pride came in many forms, he realized. Some good, some bad.

"Hey." Tom tapped the table. "Look behind you."

Frowning, Brian glanced over his shoulder. The sight of Kate at the back of the room, of her waiting for him, knocked him senseless. He moved without thinking and weaved his way around tables to reach the back of the banquet hall, then followed her into the vestibule to stand before her. He felt detached from himself as if he were clinging by his fingertips to the edge of some life-threatening precipice.

All his life he'd managed to get what he wanted by sheer willpower. This time he could only wait. What could he say? How could he explain how he'd allowed his pride to hurt both of them?

"Are you still angry?"

"No," he said softly. He wanted to take her into his arms, but he wanted more than just this moment.

"Please, don't be. Because I love you."

"Kate—"

She stepped forward and slid her arms around his waist. "I want forever with you."

All the uncertainty melted away. He tightened the embrace. "I—"

She tilted her head back and placed a fingertip to his lips. "Me, first. I'm sorry I hurt you. I was confused. So much has happened to me. I've found so much more than I'd ever hoped for. It confused me. I wanted to please them, Brian."

"I know."

"But I let that need get in the way of everything else. I love you. I don't know when it began. But I know it will never end. And that frightened me most of all. I don't want to lose you."

He tugged her closer. "You won't."

"But I nearly did because I've been afraid of the risk. Love is a risk, isn't it?"

He smiled and nodded.

"It leaves you vulnerable to hurt."

"Yes, it does," he said softly.

"But it hurts even more to love and not take that risk." She touched his cheek. "I've always been alone. Alone was safe. When you asked me to marry you, I couldn't think about anything but what I'd feel if you left me. And then you were gone." She took a deep breath. "And what I feared most I had caused. I was alone again."

"Not anymore." His mouth gently met hers. "Kate, I haven't been fair to you. When the Strantons came into your life, old ghosts returned for me. I kept letting old feelings about Diane resurface. I put pressure on you. I lied to you and to myself," he admitted.

"And that's caused us problems. If I had been straight with myself, I'd have placed few demands on you. You needed time to adjust to everything. Instead, I rushed you. I rushed you because I was afraid of losing you."

Her hand rested on his shoulder. "I suffered from a similar fear."

"You have good reasons to feel frightened. People haven't been too dependable in your life. I was the one who should have known better. But Diane left me with so much wounded pride." He gave her a wry smile. "She never loved me. That's what I hated facing. Near the end of our marriage, she admitted that. She knew her parents opposed her seeing me, and she rebelled by rushing into marriage with me. I tried to block that out." He looked away on a mirthless laugh. "Pride insisted that I run from it."

She touched his face. "I wish that I'd known."

"I wish that I'd told you. But I kept blaming her family and their wealth because I didn't want to face the truth and admit to myself that she'd made a fool of me."

Kate closed her eyes for a second as the weightiness of his confession bore down on her. "Oh, Brian." She brushed her lips against his jaw. "And still you took a chance with me and told me that you loved me."

"I had to believe that what we shared was real. I had to trust you, or we might both lose."

She rested her face against his. All her life she'd looked for an all-encompassing love, for someone who loved her. "I nearly lost you," she said raggedly as the realization swept through her.

"No. I'd never have let you go. Never," he said on a whisper so soft that she barely heard it. He drew her back and looked down at her. "You know how pushy I am."

Kate wrapped her arms tighter around his neck. "Could we leave?" she asked against his ear.

"In a few minutes. One dance first."

"And then?"

"I'll depart politely."

Gently she bit at the lobe of his ear. "But quickly?"

"Yes, quickly."

Epilogue

I'm glad I know your weaknesses," Kate said.

Brian buried his face in the pillow and groaned.

"Wake up."

He felt a kiss feather-light on the nape of his neck and peeked out of one eye. The sunlight was unbearably bright. As another kiss tickled his flesh, he opened his other eye. "I think I'm still dreaming." He felt the mattress sag as she sat on the edge of it.

"Why?"

"I smell bacon." He sniffed harder and rolled over. He caught himself gaping at the breakfast tray resting on her lap. Crisp strips of bacon framed two perfectly fried eggs. "Who...?" He looked and saw her eyes sparkling with amusement. "Not you?"

"Why not me?"

"You said that you don't cook."

"For me. I hated cooking for only me."

He pushed himself up to a sitting position, jamming pillows behind him.

"I can cook something simple like eggs."

He pressed a hand to his chest and grinned. "My heart pounds with love for you."

Kate laughed and set the tray on his lap. "Your stomach does."

He took a bite of the bacon and then offered her a taste.

"Why the serious look? Doesn't it taste good?"

"It's great."

She gave him a grim smile. "It's great," she parroted.

He met her eyes, suddenly serious. "We rushed in here last night, and I never really said everything to you that needs to be said." As she looked down, he set the tray on the table beside the bed. "About the Strantons. I know that they'll be a part of our lives." He placed a finger under her chin and forced her to look at him. "They should be."

"Yes, they should. But not like they have been. I went to see them before going to the banquet."

As she leaned forward, he felt her tremble with a sigh.

"I know they mean well, but I can't go on pleasing them to ease their consciences. I told them that I'd like to see them often, but I have a life of my own. A life that I've chosen."

He tilted his head to see her face.

"I want to see them—to be a part of their family, but I can't let them take over my life."

"Did they understand?"

She made a sound that resembled a short laugh. "They said that they did. But they weren't pleased when I turned down their offer to open my own studio.''

"You don't want it?"

She pressed her face tighter against his chest. "No."

"And Breshkov?"

"Who needs Breshkov?" She raised her face to look at him. "I like teaching at home. I like cookie time," she said on a note that sounded phony to him.

He stared hard at her. "You'd like to work with him," he said with certainty.

"Brian—"

He narrowed his eyes.

"Okay, I would have liked to work at his music academy."

She'd handled so many problems lately, he thought, touching her hand, marveling at the delicacy of it. "I—" He hesitated for only a second, sensing the anger he'd stir if he tried to protect her too much. "Where's my jacket?"

She sat back on her knees. "Why? Do you have to leave? Can't you eat breakfast first and . . ."

"There's an envelope in my jacket."

With a frown she looked over the edge of the bed. "Just a minute." She bent down and reached under his pants for his jacket.

"In the front pocket."

"Which one?"

"I don't know."

Kate flipped the jacket over and dug into first one pocket and then the other.

"When we came in last night, there was an envelope stuck in your mailbox."

"Oh, I was busy Saturday. I forgot to pick up the mail. Just one letter?"

"That's all. Were you hoping for bills?"

She punched him affectionately.

"I would have given it to you last night, but you were busy fumbling in your purse for the key." He watched her face. "And I started to hand the envelope to you but . . ."

A giggle slipped from her throat at the memory of the passion nearly unleashed before they reached her apartment door. "I remember what happened."

He said nothing as she stared at the envelope.

"Did you notice the return address?"

"Yes."

Her hand trembled as she ripped it open. "I'm glad that you didn't give this to me last night. I wouldn't have wanted anything to spoil our time together." Her fingers tightened on the small envelope.

"It looked formal."

"Breshkov is very proper." She breathed deeply as she unfolded the paper. "Even when he's rejecting someone."

When she raised her gaze, he saw a smile, the same heart-stopping one that had hooked him from the beginning.

"He wants me to audition for him again. He never gives anyone a third chance." Her voice rose with excitement. "He still might want me."

Brian touched the curve of her waist. "Smart man."

Kate pressed her hands to his chest and stared down at him. "How could he still want me? I was awful, Brian."

"You could never be awful."

"I was," she said in a voice so sincere that empathy charged through him.

"The last time?"

"Yes."

"But the first time that you played for him—" he kissed her chin "—you were brilliant."

"How do you know?"

"I listened."

"You did?"

"I listened and fell in love."

Kate rubbed her cheek against him. "Did you? Then?"

"I think so."

She smiled, looking pleased. "I guess that I shouldn't let you suffer any longer then."

"Do you have plans to ease my agony?"

Her eyes sparkled. "Many plans. But one in particular. And since you're so slow at asking the question again, I'll have to—"

"Yes."

"What do you think my question is?" she asked, placing light kisses on the curve of his neck.

"It's obvious that you'd do anything to get possession of my *Spider-man* comic collection. Even marry me."

"I'd better warn you. I want a big family."

"Yes," he said, rolling and pulling her beneath him. "We'll fill the house with kids and comic books."

"You don't want time to consider that?"

His legs moved between the slender ones that had opened in invitation to his. "Nope. We have to get started now."

"Now?"

He slid his hands around her hips. "Right now."

*   *   *   *   *

Silhouette Classics

COMING IN APRIL . . .

THORNE'S WAY by Joan Hohl

When *Thorne's Way* first burst upon the romance scene in 1982, readers couldn't help but fall in love with Jonas Thorne, a man of bewildering arrogance and stunning tenderness. This book quickly became one of Silhouette's most sought-after early titles.

Now, Silhouette Classics is pleased to present the reissue of *Thorne's Way*. Even if you read this book years ago, its depth of emotion and passion will stir your heart again and again.

And that's not all!

Silhouette Special Edition

COMING IN JULY . . .

THORNE'S WIFE by Joan Hohl

We're pleased to announce a truly unique event at Silhouette. Jonas Thorne is back, in *Thorne's Wife*, a sequel that will sweep you off your feet! Jonas and Valerie's story continues as life—and love—reach heights never before dreamed of.

Experience both these timeless classics—one from Silhouette Classics and one from Silhouette Special Edition—as master storyteller Joan Hohl weaves two passionate, dramatic tales of everlasting love!

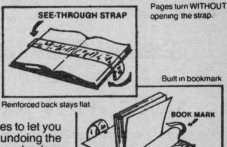

Silhouette Special Edition

NAVY BLUES
Debbie Macomber

Between the devil and the deep blue sea...

At Christmastime, Lieutenant Commander Steve Kyle finds his heart anchored by the past, so he vows to give his ex-wife wide berth. But Carol Kyle is quaffing milk and knitting tiny pastel blankets with a vengeance. She's determined to have a baby, and only one man will do as father-to-be—the only man she's ever loved...her own bullheaded ex-husband!

You met Steve and Carol in NAVY WIFE (Special Edition #494)— you'll cheer for them in NAVY BLUES (Special Edition #518). (And as a bonus for NAVY WIFE fans, newlyweds Rush and Lindy Callaghan reveal a surprise of their own....)

Each book stands alone—together they're Debbie Macomber's most delightful duo to date! Don't miss

NAVY BLUES
Available in April,
only in *Silhouette Special Edition*.
Having the "blues" was never
so much fun!
